Titche

by AJ Maloney

ISBN: 978-1-969021-22-0 (ebook)
ISBN: 978-1-969021-23-7 (Paperback)
ISBN: 978-1-969021-24-4 (Hardcover)

Library of Congress Control Number: 2025945996

Table of Contents

Dedication

This book is dedicated to the people in my day-to-day life. There is a little something in this book for or from each of them. CL, CO, JA, LG, KW, DM I'm glad you guys enjoyed it, and thanks for all your input!

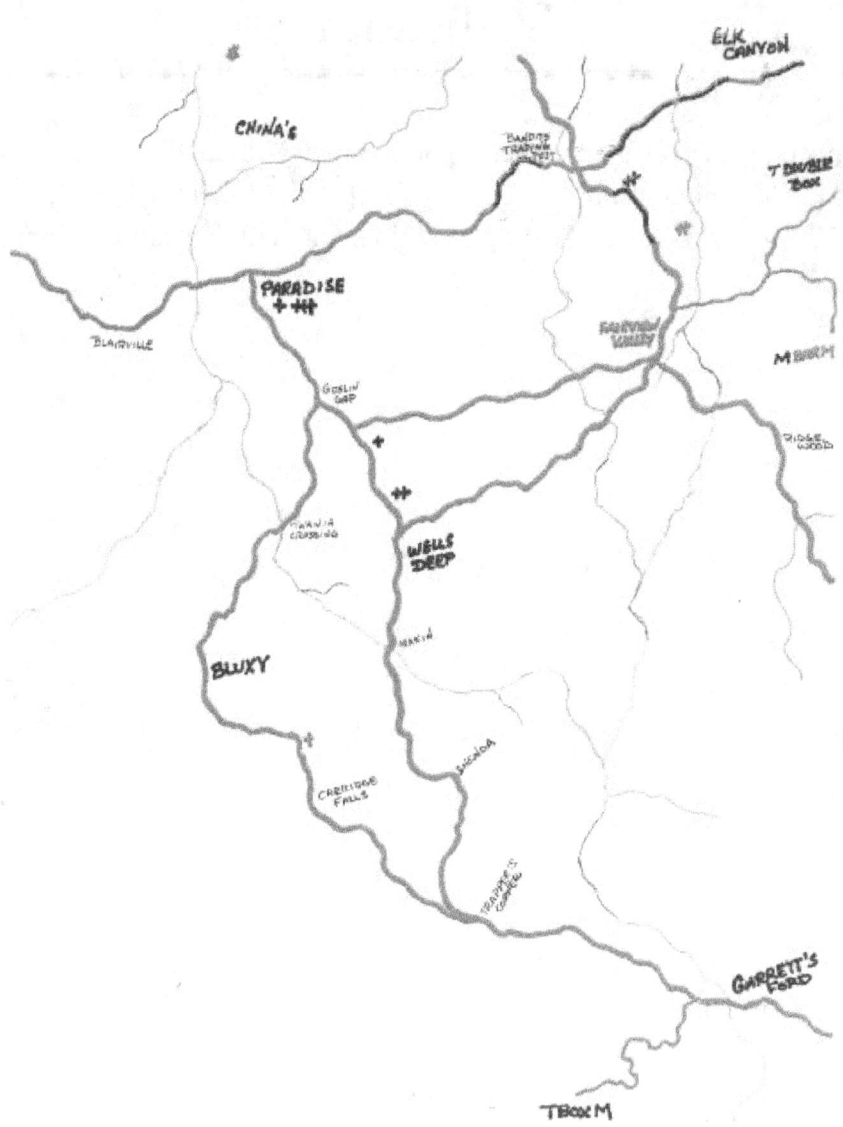

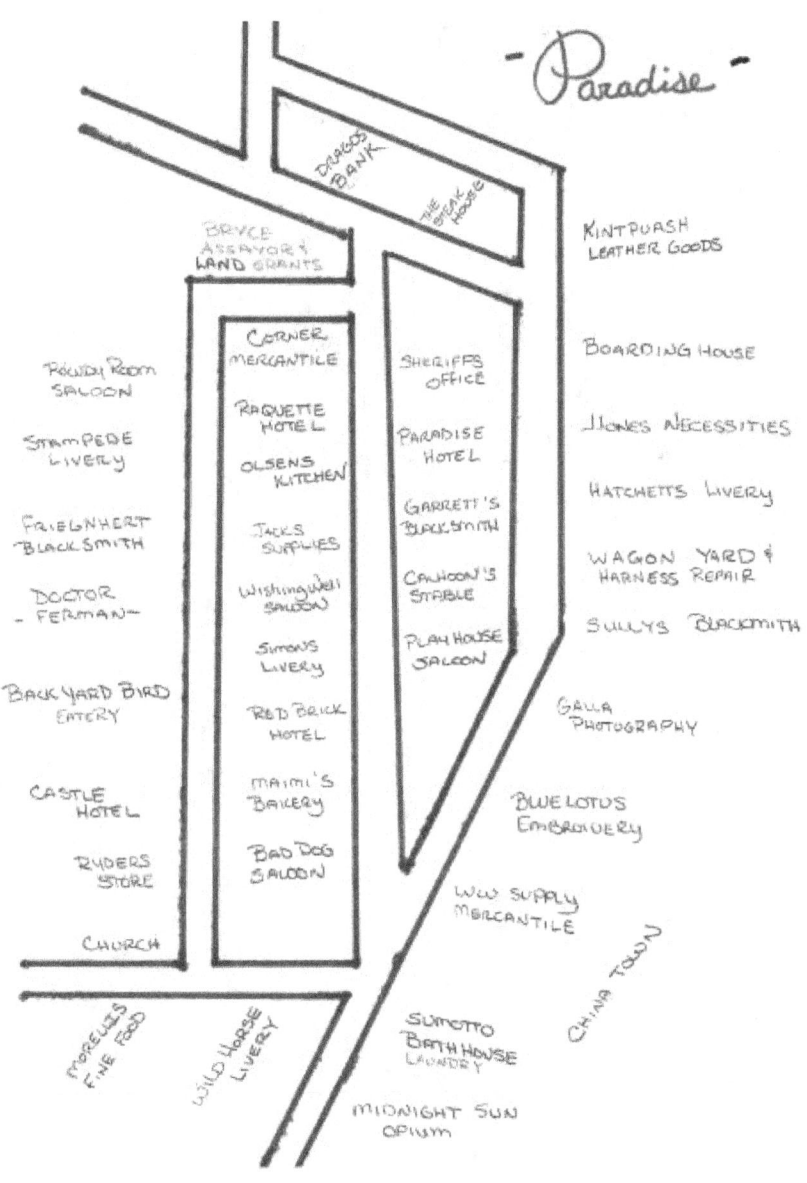

Chapter 1: Cruel Carnage

He smelled it first. The pungent odor of death. Rotting flesh accompanied by a metallic smell, which could only be a large loss of blood. Titche diverted his horse, Broken, off the trail and into a small but dense growth of pines. Hidden in the shadows, he and Broken stayed still and quiet for the better part of an hour, getting familiar with the sounds around them.

Titche considered his surroundings, going through dozens of scenarios in his mind of what might lie ahead as he sat in the shadow unseen. He also considered what his own fate could be if he didn't use extreme caution. Finally, he nudged Broken out and back onto the narrow trail, going at the slowest pace an athletic horse like Broken could manage, which was thoroughly impressive considering his stride and strength.

He and Broken had not been together a long time, but the horse was exceptionally smart and had picked up on his latest rider's needs quickly. Having traveled together through the isolated wildernesses of the northwest for just under two years, Broken could already sense his rider's moods and predict what he wanted, plus he had learned a dozen hand signals and equally as many words and sounds. This was the first rider to reward him copiously for his effort and the first rider to appreciate him. If a horse could form a thought, Broken would have considered this man to be his friend and partner. And, if a horse could form words, Broken would have told anyone he met that he would be loyal to *this* rider to the death.

The man made a small shsh sound, quick and quiet and easily missed. Broken acknowledged the sound by twisting his ears back toward his rider and then forward again. He knew this little sound meant be quiet but ready to spring into action should the need arise. Titche noted the horse's acknowledgement of his warning and rode on, easy in the saddle. He was ready to vault from the saddle if there was gunfire or the sound of a branch breaking off to the side of the trail, knowing it could mean life or death. That thought brought him back to the smell, which had grown substantially stronger.

Every sense was heightened; he was alert and ready. There was the slow, gentle sound of Broken carefully placing one foot in front of the other, the almost inaudible sound of his jeans rubbing against the leather saddle, a handful of birds high up in the tree limbs, and the hum of some bugs a few dozen feet off each side of the trail. Then he heard a new noise to the right. It was the loud buzzing of many black flies feasting on flesh.

Titche barely tightened the reins. Broken stopped immediately and went still. He certainly could smell it. Would it be beating a dead horse? Maybe a hunter's kill that had gotten away before finding a place to take its last dying breath? Titche sat eyeing the direction he must go for another thirty minutes. No one could say he was not an overly cautious man. He had good reason to be.

He gave the slightest pull on the horse's rein and leaned his weight to the right-hand stirrup. Broken gave a small shake of his head, indicating he didn't like the idea, before obediently turning in that direction.

Within a hundred feet of the trail, in a clearing of maybe ten feet in diameter, they came upon a grisly sight. Hanging by his hands from the stout limb of a hardwood tree was a young cowboy. The remnants of his campfire were long cold and his blanket was still spread on the ground next to it. There were no signs of his horse or supplies.

Titche got down and wrapped Broken's reins around his saddle horn. If the horse had to flee for any reason, he didn't want to risk the reins getting caught in his legs or in the brush. He wanted him to be able to make a clean getaway. He squatted down, not taking a single step away from the horse yet and read the scene. A young cowboy, alone. Hung up in the tree by his hands. The ropes were too tight causing them to swell and turn purple. It must have been excruciatingly painful. On the ground around him were several different boot prints of various sizes, depths, and types of boots. He could see newer boots, shallow and smaller, and hypothesized that this was a younger outlaw, maybe. Some of the boot prints were somewhere in between, different types, so were several others. Definitely a set of very large boot prints, deep, and a very worn heel. A big man, poor, maybe? It would suggest he was older, more prone to spending money on booze and whores than on clothes. Titche stood and slowly walked over to the body, watching the story play out on the ground around him. Feet traveled this way and that, leaving distinct trails that painted a picture as to who stood where, and did what, and who was friends with who… He pulled his bandana up over his mouth and nose as he coughed from the thick choking smell clogging his windpipe. His eyes raised from the ground up to the body right in front of him. There was congealed blood down his jeans, and his soaked shirt had turned dark maroon and crusty. His ankles were not tied. There were marks from the toes of his boots in the dirt where he kicked and thrashed, either trying to get some footing or from the torture. Probably both. He was shot to pieces. Bullet holes riddled every part of his body. The sons of bitches used the poor sap as target practice. None of the shots was a kill shot. They left him to hang and bleed to death out of dozens of holes. Still, as many holes as there were in him, it would not have taken him that long to die, thankfully. But that's assuming once they started shooting, they didn't stop. If they shot in stages, well, then it could have taken a very long time…

Titche scowled, his blood chilled at the cruelty of it all. He pulled a knife from his moccasin and cut the rope, letting the body fall to the ground with a loud thump. The swarm of flies followed it to the ground. He walked back to Broken and dug out an old, beat-up metal bowl. Looking for the softest spot of earth he could find, he set to scoop out a shallow grave. Once he had dragged the body by the rope to it and rolled it in, Titche set about pushing the displaced soil back onto the body. When he was done, he spread the cowboy's blanket over the new grave and collected rocks to lay on top of that. Hopefully, it was enough to keep at least some of the scavengers away, but it was not going to be any discouragement at all to something like a coyote should it happen by. Oh well. It was the best he could do for the young cowboy. He took off his hat and said out loud to the fresh grave, "I dun the best I could for ya. I hope the sons of a bitch who'r responsible fer this get what's coming to 'em. I'm going to try ta help that along. I wish I knew yer name. I would spread it through the towns in hopes that word got back to your folks. It's hard on a family, wondering what happened to their loved ones and where they lie. Now, I guess ya coulda been an outlaw yourself maybe and not deserving but, (he paused in thought) we're gonna give ya the benefit of the doubt and let bygones be bygones fer now. I'll ask God iffen he can take yer hand, but I'm not sure God and I are on the best of terms." Titche looked up at the sky. "God, I'm shur we have our differences of opinion about things and how they should be handled. But I'm asking ya to set that aside an', iffn' this young man had any good in him, ya take him by the hand ta the promised land an' help him forget his grief an' pain in his last hours. Amen."

Titche put his hat back on and took one long, last look at the boot tracks telling their stories. He felt like he knew these outlaws personally since he had spent the last couple of years studying the devastation they left along their back trail. This was a particularly cruel and clever group of men.

It took him almost a year to get this close to them. Between his extreme caution and their skill at hiding, for they, too, seemed to be extra cautious. Titche put his foot in the stirrup and swung up into the saddle. A soft squeeze of his legs and a little pressure on the reins was all Broken needed to know his rider wanted to go back to the trail, and in his mind, he was fine with that!

Back on the trail, Titche sat his horse and gazed off in the direction the outlaws were headed. He could follow and step up his pace. Broken could sure cover some ground when allowed to. He could close the gap. Visions entered his mind of the young cowboy hanging from the tree limb. He didn't want to end up like that. He didn't know this country. He didn't know what kind of ground was up ahead. Plus, he was alone against what he figured could be up to ten men, maybe. Closing the gap wouldn't undo what had already been done. "Broken, head back." He gave a slight tug on the reins and put his weight in the left stirrup. Broken twitched his ears and headed back the way they had come. Titche wanted vengeance, but he wasn't willing to die for it. The right time and the right place would come soon enough, and vengeance would be his instead of the Lord's.

Only a mile back down the trail, Titche pulled off to the side and took the bridle and saddle off Broken. He let him graze on some grass and drink from the nearby stream. When he felt the horse had gotten its fill, he put a portion of grain in his hat for it to eat.

Once that was done, he saddled back up and got back on his back trail. There was a place further along that looked most inhospitable, which he wanted to explore as a possible campsite. Everyone always looked for comfortable campsites, which was probably the cause of that poor cowboy's demise. If any of the outlaws decided to come back down the trail, they wouldn't be looking for anyone to be camping in rough terrain.

Titche came to the rocky, boulder-strewn stretch of ground he had passed several hours earlier. Getting down, he explored the area. There was a place back away, big enough for him and broken, and hidden from the trail. He would have to lead the horse across the rocky ground, staying far enough ahead to scout for rattlesnakes. Thankfully, the horse was as sure-footed as they come, or he wouldn't even have attempted it. It was slow going, but they finally reached the spot. Titche cleared some bigger stones from the ground and made enough room for him to lean against a boulder to sleep. Broken settled in and relaxed. Wrapped in his blanket, Titche chewed on some jerky from his saddlebag. It would be another cold camp in a long line of them. He would not risk smoke from a fire being seen or smelled. As he chewed and listened to the daytime sounds fade away into the distinct sounds of night, he thought about how it had all started and how far he had come.

Chapter 2: The Beginning
and the End

His parents had come west following the dream of free land and prosperity sold to them and some others by a couple of men claiming to be trail guides. A small group of families pooled their money together to hire them. They invested what little they had left over in wagons and supplies and started the long journey into the unknown. As it turned out, the trail guides were nothing more than outlaws. Several weeks out and in the middle of nowhere, they made their move to rob and kill the families, but it didn't pan out the way they had thought it would. One of the members of the small wagon train had become suspicious of them and had been talking quietly to the others. Consequently, they were prepared for the double-cross when it finally happened and killed the outlaws instead in a shootout. But now they were in a predicament. With no one to lead and no idea where they were supposed to be going, they forged ahead on their own.

As luck would have it, they ran into some honest cowboys coming back from a cattle drive. The waggoners had strayed way off course, but the cowboys brought them to a place they knew of where the families could settle. The land was rich, and game plentiful. Anybody who was willing to work hard and who could hunt had a fair chance at survival and prosperity.

Long story short, Titche's parent's dream became a reality. They made a claim to a land grant. The parcel consisted of a long valley of lush grass, a small brook, and wooded hillsides. In all, it ended up being close to six hundred acres. They built a home and barn from the timber on their own land, and they hunted their own game for food. With their first child on the way, they were careful with what supplies they still had.

The only other thing the property and the surrounding area had to offer was wild horses. Not all the horses in the herds had been *born* wild. Titche's pa got good at spotting the domesticated horses and culling them from the herds of wild horses, where he would then go about re-taming and retraining them for the sole purpose of selling them.

Settled and making a decent living, a second son was born, Titche's little brother Tolly. Out of the two boys, Titche had a special knack for horses and horse training, and the round-ups expanded to include wild-born horses. Titche would sort them out. The wild horses that didn't make the cut were branded with an X and released to breed and reproduce. Just because the parent didn't make the cut, didn't mean one of its future foals couldn't.

At a very young age, Titche was already well known for his ability to stick to and break wild broncs and for his ability in training horses. He was smart, a thinker, and a planner with disconcertingly good common-sense skills. Everyone around knew him to be a hard worker and brutally honest. He was well on his way to becoming an important and well-respected individual in the community, with his reputation already spreading to other communities.

Tolly, however, was the opposite. He had the same gift as his brother for horseflesh, but he had little interest in the backbreaking work and long hours, preferring instead to go hunting and fishing or go to town and lull on the boardwalk. Card games, whiskey, and whores at the local saloon were his only real interests as he got older, and that was where you could usually find him of an evening. He was a skillful gambler and made enough from it to support his own interests.

It wasn't long before the rift in the family became a complete split. They saw less and less of Tolly until they never saw him at all, and if by chance they passed him on the boardwalk in town, he didn't even acknowledge them. Eventually, they didn't see him at all. Tolly had moved on with his life, where and what that was, the family had no idea.

Titche wiggled against the bolder, trying to get a little more comfortable. Broken was close by, and that gave him some sense of safety and solace. He laid his head back again and closed his eyes once more. A vision of a young woman standing in the sun with laughing school children running and playing all around formed in his mind's eye.

He had been on his way to the mercantile when he saw her. He stopped his horse in its tracks and stared. She, of course, noticed and blushed. After a few minutes, she walked over and asked, "Are you just going to sit your horse and gawk or are you going to introduce yourself? My name is Annabelle, by the way." He was smitten from the moment he laid eyes on her, and as their relationship grew, it just got worse. The sun didn't rise until she did and didn't set until she went to bed. If it weren't for her, he was pretty sure the world would stop spinning and go straight to hell. His Belle was an angel straight from heaven, only walking on the ground.

It was his great honor for him to be the one she chose to marry. They built their own place not far from his parent's house, who were getting on in age. It was just the other side of the barn and corral on the same ranch, as a matter of fact. He thought it was paradise and things couldn't get any better until Anabelle informed him one morning that there would be a new addition to the family. He genuinely thought he would explode, such was the thrill of the news, and seven months later, his son Jacob was born. The first time he held his own baby in his arms, his heart grew ten times bigger. Life was perfect.

Titche made a small sigh in his sleep. Broken opened his eyes to check on his rider. Seeing he was asleep, he shut his own eyes again.

Hours later and deep into the night, another vision formed in his tortured dreams. It was about the day he had come back from driving some horses south to a buyer. He knew instantly something was wrong. The sun was shining, but the ranch was still and quiet. His aging father was not puttering or rocking on the porch. His aging mother was not hanging laundry with his wife or gardening. The corral was empty of horses, and the gate was wide open.

He jumped down from his horse and ran to his parents' house first since it was closest. Inside, he found his father tied to a chair. There were so many knife cuts from his ankles up that he didn't think he could count them all. He had been scalped as well, and it sat on the table by him like a discarded toupee. Flies buzzed, and one crawled out of his mouth, which hung open. Vile filled his stomach and throat. He almost retched then and there. Annabelle came to mind with thoughts of his mother right on her heels. He turned and ran outside. He would cut through the barn, which was the quickest way to get to his own house.

He did not expect the scene that greeted him when he entered its cool, dim interior. His mother and his wife hung naked from the rafters by their hands, which were puffy and purple. Their toes barely touched the barn floor, and the hay had been kicked clear by their struggling, swinging feet. The bare boards of the barn floor were stained with their dried blood. Both were shot to pieces. Flies gathered at the holes piercing their torsos. Tears pooled in his eyes and slid down his cheeks in hot trails. He wasn't sure how long he had stood there before he thought of his son Jacob. He snapped out of it and ran for his own house on the far side of the barn.

Inside was cool and neat, blue lacy curtains fluttered with the slight breeze. A pot of stew was still on the cookstove. A half-eaten bowl of it was on the table with a baby bottle close at hand. Near the table was a wooden cradle. Titche walked over and reluctantly looked in. He saw his small son's body, only a few months old, with a towel over his tiny face. He had been smothered.

Titche let out a loud wail deep from within his soul and collapsed to his knees. Great gasps wracked his lungs so hard that he thought his ribs would surely break, and his head spun at a dizzying speed until blackness dimmed out the light and, blessedly, took over.

He moaned in his sleep. Broken opened his eyes. He took a couple of steps closer to his rider, putting his nose close to his face, his nostrils flared with several deep breaths. He was asleep, but the horse could tell it was not a good sleep. He stayed awake for a while until his rider's breathing evened out and he seemed to be more relaxed. Then Broken relaxed again and was able to rest until morning finally came.

Chapter 3: Back Trail

Titche was awakened by Broken, who nudged him. He didn't move, but he did open his eyes. The horse's face was close to him, and he was giving him "the stare". It always meant that he had heard something he thought his rider should know about, so Titche sat up carefully and listened. After several minutes of silence, he slowly stood. Leaning against the boulder, he kept listening. Broken stood looking to the right, ears perked. It was several more minutes before Titche heard the sound of hooves some distance down the trail. He looked Broken in the eye. Putting his hand on his muzzle, he said quickly and quietly, "shsh" before disappearing around the boulder.

He moved stealthily, getting closer to the trail but not wanting to get too close where either the horses would notice him or the men riding. He found another spot tucked in behind some large rocks that were bunched up, where he could get in and squat down. He was about half the distance back to the trail now from where Broken remained hidden in the boulders. He listened as the horses drew closer. Two men were talking, and he could make out what they were saying.

"Trey, I'mma tellin' ya. There's someone trailin' us and has been fer months."

"Riff, no one trails a bunch for months on end jus ta not confront 'em. What'cha sayin makes no damn sense."

"Yeah, well how do ya explain that there cow-punch getting cut down and burreed? He buries himself, ya horse's ass?"

There was a pause before 'Trey' responded. "I'll grant ya that. Someone did burry 'im fer sure. But it doesn't mean they were trailin' us in-particular. They coulda happened on him."

"Nope. We're fer shur bein' trailed."

"Then whar ta hell is he! An' why would he jus' trail us and not do nothin' about it? It don't make sense, Riff."

The two riders were level with Titche and slowly passing by. He took a cautious look. One was young and apparently this was Trey. The other was maybe ten years older. That would be Riff.

Seeing no response coming from his comrade, Trey went on, "We checked all the good camp spots up to where we had some sport with that fella. Nothin'. Now we are back-trailin' a back-trailer? He wouldn't'a backtrailed hisself! This jus makes no plum damn sense atall."

Riff sighed. "It don't make sense. None of it. Which is why I'm as uneasy as a jackrabbit in a field. I don't like it that this turd kin disappear like smoke on a windy day. I wanna know whar the bastard is and why he's a-trailin us. He's a-got me right down paranoid, and there's no way in hell I can take another month of it."

"I'm trying ta tell ya, Riff, no one has been trailin us, much less fer months. No one does somethin' like that."

"Let's make it to where the stream crosses the trail. Then we'll turn around and catch up with the rest of the boys. We'll be back with the bunch by tomorrow evenin'. But I'm telling ya hard, we're being stalked like wolves on a deer."

"OK, OK. A lil further. Turn around an' head back." Trey paused a minute before adding, "Finally."

They were well past Titche's hiding spot. He made his way quickly and quietly to the edge of the trail and looked up and down it. About twenty feet in the direction the two men had ridden was a large overgrown bush. He quickly made his way to it and found a spot that, with minimal effort, he could get under. He pulled the left Bowie knife from his Moccasin and clenched the blade in his teeth. This was one of those rare chances to dispense a little justice.

He heard the horses coming back up the trail.

"Yeah, well, Jule never showed back up did he?" It was 'Riff's' voice.

"Maybe he decided ta quit the bunch an' didn't wanna tell us. Maybe he wanted ta git somewhere different." Trey could hear the doubt in his own voice.

"Nah. Iff'n yer gonna quit, ya usually do it in the next town. We was only a week out from Bluxy. He said he was gonna let that lame horse of his rest a day or two an' he'd see us in thar. We was in that shithole town a week an' he never showed. Im'ma tellin' ya, shur as a cat chasin' a mouse, that man trailin' us got 'im. That would be *exactly* why he didn't show up."

The riders were even with Titche, and he snaked out from under the bush as quick as any sidewinder. He grabbed Riff by the back of his coat and pulled him off his horse. By the time he hit the ground, Titche had already reached around with his left hand and sliced his throat open from ear to ear.

Meanwhile, Trey pulled his horse to a sharp stop next to Riff's now empty saddle. "What gives, Riff? Ya fall smack offn' yer horse or what?" He had been looking the other way when the incident occurred and was confused by what had happened to cause Riff to topple from his saddle. There hadn't been a gunshot, which was Trey's first thought, being an outlaw and all.

14

Titche came around the front of Riff's horse in a crouch. He stood straight up and threw both hands hard up in the air in front of Trey's mount, causing him to rear up and throw his unsuspecting rider. Trey toppled off the back and hit the ground hard. Air whooshed out of his lungs, and for a moment, he was breathless and stunned.

Titche was on him, Bowie poised to drive into him. Trey grabbed his wrist and wrenched it enough that the deadly knife sank into the trail dirt. With as much force as he could muster, he swung, and Titche took a hard right to his jaw. It knocked him sideways and onto his back. Trey jumped to his feet and went for his gun, but Titche was already in a crouched position and dove at Trey's thighs, knocking him back against a tree. Trye drove his elbow down into Titche's shoulder, and he let go and backed up. The two men eyed each other for a minute.

"You should have paid more attention to your compadre, amigo diablo."

"Yer the joker trailin' us?" Trey went for his gun again. But Titche lunged sideways and grabbed a long, broken branch hanging from a tree next to the trail. He ripped it the rest of the way down and swung with force as Trey's pistol came up. It was a direct hit to his gun hand. Bones cracked, and the gun flew into the bushes. Trcy howled with pain. "Why, you son of a no good whore!" He charged Titche, and when he swung the branch again at his head, Trey ducked, but Titche brought it right back low and took Trey's feet out from under him. Trey hit the ground and rolled, coming up next to Titche's Bowie, sticking up out of the dirt. He grabbed it. Back on his feet, he was crouched and waiting for Titche's next move. It was Titche's turn to charge. Try slashed the Bowie at him, intending to liberate his guts from the rest of him, but Titche's arm came up from underneath in a half-circle motion and sent the slice upward harmlessly into the air. Trey landed a left to the side of Titche's face, but it was a glancing blow as he had seen it coming and leaned back. But even so, a small cut opened near his eye, and a droplet of blood slid down. Meanwhile, Titche was able to land a solid right into the outlaw's solar plexus as well as a left to his face. Trey staggered sideways, but he wasn't done yet. He had spent a lifetime scrapping. He raced to get behind Titche and strike with the Bowie, intending to bury it in his kidney. But instead, Titche twirled to his left, and he was the one behind Trey instead. He wrapped his forearm around the outlaw's neck, choking him. Trey slashed it with the Bowie. Titche let go, blood running down his arm. They faced off again, crouched and circling each other. Trey charged again with the Bowie held low. He was going to bring it up in a powerful stroke and slice this bastard from stem to sternum. Unexpectedly, Titche stepped closer and, with equal force, brought his forearm up hard under the swing. The knife blade tore his shirt, and the tip barely cut a path up Titche's ribs. As Trey's arm flew upwards out of control, Titche pulled the other Bowie from his other moccasin and plunged it into Trey's belly. His eyes widened in shock and pain. Titche shoved him hard backwards, and the knife came free as he fell. Trey's fingers relaxed, and the Bowie he was holding rolled out of his grasp. Titche picked it up. He plunged both knives into the dirt to get some of the blood off before putting them back into each of his moccasins.

Titche saw the question form in the dying outlaw's eyes even though it could not form on his lips. "This is fer my parents, my wife, my son, an' my ranch, ya sorry cocksucker! This is fer the countless others, some of whom I came along behind ya an' gave a proper burial. I'm plenty sorry fer the ones out there who *didn't* get buried." By the time he finished, the light went out of Trey's eyes. He stared blankly at Titche's face.

Trey and Riff had met as young cow punchers, still wet behind the ears, for an outfit in Arkansas that ended up going bust a couple of years later. It was during a time when any kind of job was hard to find.

Starving, they robbed a stagecoach and got a decent payday. The intention was for it to only be once, but one thing led to another. Any memories they had of the days when they were 'good 'ole boys' had long since faded into obscurity. Now they had died together in equal obscurity. They would not be remembered, and their bodies, left in the elements to be ravaged, would never be found.

He dragged the dead outlaws quite some distance off the trail after tying the horses to a nearby tree. He left them to the scavengers. Men like them deserved less, if it were possible. Back on the trail, he crossed over it and made his way back to his own horse. He got himself ready to move out and left as little evidence of his stay as was possible. Very carefully, he led Broken back through the rocks and onto the trail. He broke a branch off an evergreen tree and brushed the trail where the fight took place. Then he grabbed handful after handful of dirt, tossing it up in the air and letting it come down. "Two more down, Broken. But we will have to start from scratch again. It's OK, though. We have nothing else to do."

He untied the outlaws' horses and attached a lead rope. With one last look to make sure he wiped out as much of the evidence of the fight as he could, he started down his back trail. The outlaws might have made some wrong assumptions about the man he now knew was called Jules, but he didn't think they would make that mistake again. One missing member was one thing, but now it would be three missing members. If the other outlaws didn't start to suspect on their own, Riff would have put the notion into their heads by checking their back trail. The rest of the bunch would probably be a bit more jumpy in the future when these two didn't return.

He didn't want to let these horses loose for fear they would head back to wherever the bunch was holding up. Then they would know instantly and for sure that they had a problem. If he took the horses back to Wells Deep, someone there might recognize the horses and remember the riders. They would wonder why he had them and why the saddles were empty, and they would no doubt note the man bringing them in and leaving them.

If the outlaws decided to try to find out what happened to their pards, they would probably follow the trail all the way back to town. That is, if they didn't discover the bodies out in the woods or notice his tracks leaving the trail. They would find the horses at the stable and ask questions if he brought them back to the last town. The hostler would be able to give them a description of the man who brought the horses back and what he rode. He couldn't have that. Anonymity was his friend.

A way back, there was a fork in the trail. Instead of going all the way back to Wells Deep, the last town, he would take the fork and see where it led. He would keep the horses with him until he could find a place to leave them somewhere along the way. The greater the distance between him and these outlaws for a while, the better. The longer he could keep them confused and guessing about their missing compadres, the better. His goal was to even up the odds slowly. The longer they went without knowing what he looked like or riding for a horse, the safer he would be. It would take considerable time to cross their trail again in the future, but it would be worth it in the long run. Time was all he had anymore, anyway.

Chapter 4: Fairview Valley

Two weeks later, Titche sat hidden under some low-lying limbs in a stand of trees bordering a small town. The trail he had taken had led northeast and eventually met up with a wider, much more traveled road. At first, Titche went south, blending his horses' tracks in with those of other travelers. A day later, he found a good place to step off the trail where they would not leave tracks, so he did and turned the horses North again, keeping them parallel with the road but not on the road. A few days after that and well past the spot where he had originally entered the road and turned south, he eased back on the road again, heading North this time and blending their tracks in again with any others. It had only been a few hours of riding when he saw the small town in the distance. Since then, he had sat quietly and watched people come and go. It was like any other small Western town. Nothing stood out about it.

At dusk, he rode in, leading the two outlaws' horses. He headed for the stable.

Clap was sitting with the back of his chair leaning against the barn wall, the front legs a few inches off the ground. He watched the stranger coming along the street slowly, leading two horses. When he was in front of the barn door, Clap let his chair fall back down on all four legs and stood up. "Howdy, stranger. How kin I hep ya?" He scrutinized the man in front of him openly because he didn't need to be saddled with any trouble. As far as he could tell, this man was in his mid-thirties, maybe, with a very direct gaze. There was no softness in his hazel eyes, nor around his mouth. He was tanned from the sun, dark curls clung and rubbed against the underside of his hat brim and neck. He had a colt tied down low on his thigh, and it looked recently oiled. There was a Bowie handle sticking out of each moccasin. He guessed him to be about six feet and *maybe* 230 pounds, but none of it was fat. He sat his horse well, indicating someone who spent a lot of time in the saddle. The horses looked to be in excellent shape, well taken care of. That spoke well of the stranger, but the empty saddles on the horses with him gave him pause.

Titche let the hostler size him up first before answering.

"I'm lookin' ta stable an' grain my horses."

Clap rubbed his chin. "Whar are yer friends?"

"Outlaws. Six feet under." He didn't know how this little man would take it, that his friends were six feet under, or the outlaws were six feet under, and these were *their* horses.

"That's tough," Clap said when he finally got around to it. He didn't really know what this stranger meant by that, but it was considered rude to question a man too much, so he let it go. "I got room. It'll cost ya. I charge five dollars a day, but I double grain, an' they al'us have fresh hay an' water. Stalls are so clean ya could eat offn' the floor!"

Titche chuckled. "Never been one ta eat offn' a floor, no matter how clean it was. Fair enough, I guess. He reached inside his duster and pulled out a double eagle and flipped it through the air to the hostler, who caught it deftly in his left hand. "That'll take care of the next few days, I believe."

Clap watched as Titche swung down from his horse. It was smooth and graceful, with no wasted motion. He kept one hand free, not far from his colt. Now that he was standing on the ground, Clap could see a second colt tucked away in his waistband. This man was loaded for bear. He felt a little nervous all of a sudden. He looked again at the empty saddles.

"If ya tell me where ya want 'em, I'll put 'em up an' give 'em a good rubdown."

"Bring 'em on in an' ya kin have yer pick of the stalls. My name is Clap, by the way. I'll get their grain rations to 'em here shortly. I usually do it after dinner."

"I surely appreciate it, Clap. I'm Titche. Dinner sounds good. Where does one eat in this town?"

"Oh, well we don't actually have a real eatery here, yet anyway. But iffn' ya go ta the end of the street an' left, you'll see a little white house. It belongs to Miss Mabel. She loves to cook, an' so she has taken ta make'n a sizable amount of food and selling it at a dollar a plate. Kinda an unofficial eatery. Ya kin get breakfast, lunch, or dinner dependin' on when yer there, an' when ya leave, ya damn sure won't be hungry anymore!" Clap chuckled. "She sure is a fine cook. I thought about proposin' ta her just so's I kin get good free vittles fer the rest of my days!" He laughed and slapped his knee at his own joke. Titche chuckled at his humor as he stripped the horses down. He took a small brush from his saddlebag and started brushing down the first horse. Clap was surprised. "Well, I'll be coon's cousin. I haven't seen anyone more'n rub their horse down with handfuls of hay in a dog's age."

"I grew up on a horse ranch. It relaxes me ta take the time ta do it. Helps the horse ta relax too. No reason fer a man ta not take care of his mount. Especially out here where a man really needs ta depend on one."

"Ya shur are arrow straight about that."

"Anything else I should know about this town of yours, Clap?"

Clap blinked. "What'cha mean by that? An' it's not really *my* town…"

"I mean, do I have to worry about hotheads or outlaws riding through?"

"Oh! No, Sir, Mr. Titche! Fridee an' Saturdee night the boys from the M Bar M and the T Double Box ranches come in an' kick up the dust a little, but they is all a good bunch o' cow pokes. No trouble t'all really. Strangers here are few an' far between."

"Yer indeed blessed then."

"I don't know about that. Slim pickins at making a living out here."

"Ya don't have outlaws shootin' up yer town, raping yer women folk, an' robbing ya blind like some of ta'other towns on down the trails."

Clap cringed. He had forgotten about the empty saddles. "Yep, Mr. Titche, ya shur got me there. I hadn't thought about it. Sorry. We definitely kin be thankful fer that blessin'." Clap patted one of the other horses Titche had brought with him. He wanted to ask exactly what happened, but it was pure bad manners, and his momma raised him better.

"Ya got a sheriff here?"

"No, sir. But all of the townsfolk kin handle a weapon of one kind or other. They settled this place, ya know. It hasn't been so long that they've forgotten what it means ta fight fer yer home."

Titche left that stall and moved on to the next one. Stripping the horse down and then methodically starting to brush its coat.

Clap took note and went to the third stall and stripped that one down himself for Titche. He heard the man mumble "Much obliged" from the other stall. Clap rubbed his hand over the horse he was standing next to. It was a fine animal, really. "If ya don't mind me askin', what're ya plannin' ta do with these horses?"

Titche was quiet for a few minutes before answering. "I don't rightly know, Clap. I couldn't leave them out there in the wilds. I don't know who they belong ta iff'n anybody at'tal. I would sell 'em ta someone who needs 'em an' would take good care of 'em but I don't know anyone around here. I guess, iffn' I ever make it back ta my ranch, I could release 'em an' let 'em mingle with the wild horse herds fer a spell. New blood." He knew the last part of that would never happen. He would most likely never see his ranch again. It wasn't even his anymore if his foggy memory served him right. He could feel the knife drive into his heart and twist.

"Well, I might have an answer fer ya! We don't get any horsetraders here. I believe either one of the ranches would probably buy 'em from ya as long as no one's lookin' for 'em that is."

Titche left the stall he was in and came into the stall where Clap stood, still rubbing his hand along the horse's back. "They would treat 'em kindly? Which ranch would take the best care of 'em? They've earned some pamperin'."

"Oh, either one. Real stand-up ranchers, both of 'em. The kind ta ride the river with."

Titche kept methodically brushing the third horse. "What's today, Clap?"

"Why it's Tuesdee."

"Is there a place fer me ta lay my head? Get a hot bath drawn?"

"If ur not agin' it, you'd have ta stay at the saloon. They'd likely give ya a room since business is slow durin' the week. Lucille would pour ya a hot bath an' a cut fer a price."

Titche grinned as he looked across the horse's back at Clap. "I must be lookin' pretty shaggy then."

Clap looked uncomfortable. "I'm sorry about that. I didn't mean to imply…" Titche raised his hand.

"It's OK, Clap. I'm sure I could use a trim by now."

A bell rang down the street. Clap's head spun towards the sound. He looked back at Titche with excitement. "That's the dinner bell! Mable is done cookin'! It's first come, first serve Mr. Titche so's I wouldn't be draggin' my feet getting' down there."

"OK, Clap. Thanks. I'll be right along. I'm mostly done here."

Clap was out of the stall and out of the barn door before Titche could say dinnertime.

Another ten minutes and he was done brushing down the last horse. Titche headed out the door and down the street, too.

Mable's little white house wasn't hard to find, and even if it had been, the smell of slow-cooked beef would have been enough to lead you right to it. Wooden tables were set up outside. There was already a fair number of people sitting in groups here and there, talking and laughing. Titche spotted Clap, who motioned for him to come over and pointed to a plate piled high with beef smothered in gravy, with potatoes and corn on the side. A loaf of freshly made bread sat in the middle of the table with a few substantial chunks already cut from it. Titche went over and sat down. It wasn't a full minute when a heavy-set woman, her face flushed from the heat of the kitchen, came over to stand by the table. Wiping her hands on her apron, she said, "You must be Titche. It's a dollar a plate, and ya don't leave hungry. If that isn't enough to fill ya along with a slice of pie and double cups of coffee, I will find something more for ya in the cupboards."

Titche smiled up at her and dug out some coins from his jean pockets, handing her a dollar. "Nice ta meet ya miss Mable. I'm sure a black bear wouldn't be able ta shove another mouthful down his gullet after all that!" She looked pleased by the compliment.

"It's just Mable, Titche, and thank'ye kindly for sayin so!" Then she disappeared back into the house for more plates of food for some folks who were just arriving and sitting down

Clap was right. The food was absolutely delicious, and when he swallowed the last bite of his pie, washed down by the last swallow of his second cup of coffee, he had no room left for more. She meant it when she said no one leaves hungry.

Clap was busy eating, not talking, and pretty much inhaled his food. As soon as he was done, he jumped up from the table and set off for the barn to grain the horses.

Titche had eaten slowly so as to enjoy every bite. It was a treat to get a hot, home-cooked meal. Mostly, he had cold camps consisting of jerky and water. He would not risk a fire while he was on the trail of outlaws. He was one of the last ones to leave. He strolled along the street back towards the stable and entered the saloon. That was all the sign said. He wondered if the owner had even bothered to name it.

A balding man was wiping down the bar. No one else was inside.

"What kin I get ya?"

"Maybe a room an' a hot bath fer a couple of nights?"

"Yep. That could be arranged but not fer Fridee and Saturdee night."

"I hope ta be gone by then."

Two women came down the stairs. The bar owner asked for one of them to draw up a hot bath. The younger of the two headed towards the back of the saloon. The other one came over to stand beside Titche.

"You're new. Need some company?"

"No, ma'am. Travel worn. I could use a hot bath, a trim, an' a good night's sleep."

"No one calls me 'mam'. My name's Lucille." She looked him up and down slowly with experienced eyes. "And that's a cryin' shame, mister. Maybe you'll feel differently in the morning."

He smiled but did not accept the offer. Instead, he asked, "Are ya the one ta ask fer a trim?"

"I'm a fair shake at it, if ya ain't too fussy."

"I'm not."

"Then follow me, Mister. We'll see what ya really look like once you're cleaned up."

He tossed a double eagle on the bar as he started to follow Lucille to the back room.

"I'll have some change fer ya when yer done back there."

Titche nodded.

The hot bath felt splendid. He relaxed and soaked while Lucille trimmed his black curls back to a respectable length. After she was done, she left a straight razor and a mirror near the tub. Looking down at him, she shook her head slowly. "*Damn* shame ya don't feel up ta some company, Mister." Titche smiled. He had never had any problem getting a woman to notice him, and even though he had been a long time on the owl hoot trail, apparently, he still didn't. He picked up the razor and mirror and started to shave. Lucille sashayed out of the room. The man looking back at him from the mirror looked older and grimmer. His eyes had turned harder, and the smile lines around his lips had faded away.

Out of the tub and dressed again, he returned to the bar and grabbed his change.

"I already paid the girls fer the bath an' cut."

"Appreciate it kindly."

"Last room at the end of the hall upstairs. It has a door an' back stairs so ya can come and go in private."

"Again, appreciate it."

Titche went to the stable and got his belongings out of the stall where his horse was lounging. Broken nickered to him when he saw him come in. "I know, boy. I'll be fine. Git yerself some well-deserved pamperin'." He stopped at each of the other two stalls and gave them each some attention as well. He noted that clean water and fresh hay were available for the horses as promised.

Back at the saloon, he went around back and found the stairs leading up to the second story and a door. He climbed them, found the door unlocked, and went in. The room was cleaner and tidier than he had expected. He set his gear down, stripped, and lay on the bed. Some might find the bed too hard, but any kind of bed, hard or soft, was a treat to him. He could count on one hand how many times he had slept in a bed over the last several years. He could hear the clinking of glasses and bottles of whiskey downstairs. Other than that, the town was pretty quiet. He felt the ugly demon in him urging him to go have a drink, but he knew better. It had gotten hold of him once, but he wouldn't let it happen again. At least, not until he had killed every one of the savages that had destroyed his family and life. The light sound of glass gently tapping more glass lulled him into a fitful sleep. Memories chased each other behind closed eyes.

Chapter 5: A Trail of Empty Bottles

Titche's collapse from a respected businessman and ranch owner to a defeated and disgraced drifter and drunk started many years before.

A rough bunch had ridden into town and were kicking up their heels at the local saloon. The sheriff had spent the evening holding up a post with his shoulder. With his thumbs tucked in his gun belt, he watched the goings-on through the swinging saloon doors across the muddy road. While they made a lot of ruckuses and had a few shoving matches, they kept their irons holstered. It surprised him. He didn't like the looks of them and was sure each one was wanted for something somewhere. There was nothing he could arrest them for, though, and he didn't see any of these mugs on his wanted posters at the office. He kept a close eye on them anyway for most of the evening.

He was thankful when they rode out the next day. But before they rode out, while on his way to breakfast, the sheriff had looked over their horses. He was surprised to see one of them, a truly beautiful black and white Paint, had an X branded on its rump. That was the brand the horse ranch across the ford put on some of the horses they released back into the wild after a round-up. He couldn't imagine this horse ever being released back once it was caught, though. It was a curious thing. He decided that he would ride out to the ranch when he got a chance and ask them about it.

A couple of days later, he saw Titche ride through. He was headed for home after delivering some horses that he had sold down south.

He would have gone out and flagged him down, but he was busy listening to one of the church women. She demanded he do something about young Danial Sully, who was picking the flowers out of the church garden to give to his mother. Sheriff Benz tried to reason with her that he was young and trying to do something nice for his mamma, but she wasn't having any of it. "Children need discipline and to be taught manners, Sheriff Benz, or the world will end up in chaos." He finally agreed to have a talk with the young boy, which he did. He told him that it was a very nice thing he had done for his mother and that next time, he should come over and pick some of his wife's flowers from her garden because they were prettier. The boy giggled, showing his missing front tooth. His wife wouldn't mind a lick if the boy picked every last flower for his mother. She said it was what flowers were intended for in the first place.

That is how the sheriff ended up out at the horse ranch shortly after Titche. He was the one who found him, loaded him into a wagon, and brought him back to town to be seen by the doc right away. He told the doc what he saw and how he found Titche unconscious. Doc Spencer looked him over and declared there were no injuries. "He is suffering from shock."

Titche eventually woke up. He was disoriented. When the doctor came in to check on him, he asked what had happened. "Did I get thrown from my horse or something?"

Doc Spencer scrutinized him from under bushy white eyebrows. "Much worse than that, I'm afraid."

"What do ya mean, Doc?"

"It'll come to you, young man. Right now, get some more rest."

Titche slept most of the day and all of the night. But when he woke up the following morning, he remembered everything. Doc rushed in when he heard the wail from the other room. Titche was on his knees beside his bed with his head in his hands, wailing. Doc Morton turned around and left, giving him privacy, and went to find the sheriff. They spent some time talking about it and what was best to do for Titche. And, of course, they wanted to give him some time to grieve before talking with him. It was a little over an hour before they headed back to the doctor's office.

When they went inside, they found Titche gone. Sheriff Benz ran to the livery to saddle his horse but saw that Titche's mount was still in the stable. Henry, the hostler, hadn't seen Titche at all. The sheriff turned around and slowly walked the boardwalk, trying to think of where Titche might have gotten to. As he was passing the saloon, he glanced inside and there sat Titche, already halfway through a bottle of gut-rot. He went in and sat next to him. Neither one spoke for a while.

Finally, the sheriff spoke first. "I know 'sorry' doesn't cover it, Titche. That was an evil I have never seen nor heard of that happened out there to your family. I want you to know, the town went out and we took care of your loved ones real proper like. We picked a beautiful knoll and put the tent together. It's sunny and has a beautiful view of the ranch. The womenfolk cleaned the houses and put things away for ya."

Titche didn't speak. He just poured and downed another shot.

"Titche, you should probably ease up on that some." Sheriff Benz felt guilty even saying it. He would probably be doing the same thing if what had happened to Titche's family had happened to his wife and daughter.

Titche poured another shot and downed it again.

The sheriff sighed. "I have to ask you something. There was a rowdy bunch in town. They didn't cause enough trouble for me to arrest them for anything. I don't know that it's they who did what was done. But one of those men rode a very striking horse, and you know horse flesh." Titche didn't act like he even heard him. He continued to speak anyway. "It was a mighty fine black and white Paint. It had a peculiar brand on its back end. You know any horse like that?"

Titche poured another shot and watched it swirl around in the shot glass a few times before he swallowed it.

The sheriff stared hard at him. "It had an X on it like the ones your ranch puts on some of those wild horses you don't want to catch again. But, I'm purty sure you wouldn't of let that one go back. It was a fine specimen of a horse for sure enough."

Titche put down the shot glass and drank what was left straight from the bottle.

"I'm asking you, Titche, did you ever brand a horse like that? A fine black and white Paint? Do you ever change your mind about any of the horses you brand with an X and release? Could you tell me anything about an hombre riding a horse like that?"

Titche didn't answer. His chin sank to his chest, and his eyes closed. If the sheriff hadn't reached out and grabbed his arm, he would have toppled from the bar stool and landed on the sawdust floor. The barkeep came around the bar and between the two of them, they got him upstairs and laid him out on one of the beds.

That was the end of the Titche everyone knew and respected. Every day was more of the same until he had run out of money in his pockets, run out of horses to sell, and had sold the ranch. Everyone was sick of him. He was an embarrassment and a nuisance. The town demanded that Sheriff Benz run him out, and finally, he had no other option but to do just that. With a heavy heart, he dragged Titche out of the saloon, put him on the last horse he had to his name, and with a slap on the rump, told him to get gone. He wasn't welcome anymore.

And so, it was for Titche, town after town, until they no longer wanted him mucking stalls or sweeping boardwalks for pocket change to buy shots with.

A new town, a different sheriff, saying the same thing the rest had. Titche didn't know his name. He didn't even know which town this one was.

"You've overstayed your welcome, Titche. You need to go. People are getting riled."

"I can't leave. I've got no money, and I've got no horse."

The sheriff knew deep down that this man was not a bad man. He had probably even been something once. But, sure as goose shit is slippery, he wasn't in a good place now. "I'll be back in a minute. Don't wander off." The sheriff walked down to the corral and came back with what had to be the oldest pony alive. He dropped the reins and went into the saloon. He came back out shortly, carrying a bottle of gut-rot. "Come on over here and mount up, Titche. She's old, almost blind, and probably deaf. Treat her good, though, and she might get you to the next town down the line." Titche mounted up, swaying some in the saddle. "Here's some whiskey to get ya there."

"Much obliged."

"I'm not sure I would consider this a favor, Titche." He gave the pony a slap on the ass, and it slowly moved forward and down the trail, going out of town. The sheriff thought to himself, I believe that pony knows they are both being put out to pasture. If God needs to go with anybody, it's those two.

Chapter 6: The Chinaman

That pony lasted longer than anyone would have guessed. But boy, did she get them lost. Two weeks later, they were on a faint trail that could only lead to hell, thought Titche. His head ached endlessly. He shook so bad; he had a hard time pissing without getting it all over himself. Sweat rolled off him despite the chill in the mountain air. All of a sudden, the little pony went crashing down, and Titche found himself pinned. She was lying on his leg, and he couldn't pull it out. Little Bessie, as he had begun to call her, was stone-cold dead. Try as he might, he couldn't get loose. Finally, he gave up. He lay there on the trail, watching puffy white clouds float by in a brilliant blue sky. He thought to himself, this is the end of it all.

But it wasn't. As he stared up at the clouds, waiting to be released from this life, a face leaned over and looked down at him. He thought he just *had* to be hallucinating because there was a Chinaman looking down at him on the path to hell. It was almost funny. Then the face was gone. Titche turned his head and saw the man looking over the dead horse.

He watched as the Chinaman walked around, peering into the woods here and there before finally coming back over to the dead horse. He took a knife from his garment. Titche thought to himself, if he tries ta cut off my leg, I'm gonna kill him. Instead, the Chinaman shoved the knife into the horse's abdomen and proceeded to gut it. He's gonna eat the horse, thought Titche. It took most of an hour, but the Chinaman finally got the horse dressed out. With that done, he came back around to Titche and grabbed him under his arms. He pulled, and Titche could feel his leg start to come out from under what was left of the body of poor Bessie, and with it, excruciating pain. His last thought before he blacked out was, I'll be damned. He lightened the load.

When Titche came to, he was lying on a cot in a very small shack. His cot was against a wall on his right, and to his left was a fire pit in the corner of that wall. A door opened outward at the foot of the cot. Against the far wall, on the dirt floor, was some kind of sleeping mat. It was at a right angle to the cot he was in. There was a pile of black pebbles thrown in the corner haphazardly between the top of the mat and the same wall that the fire pit was on. He looked down his body at the leg that had been caught under the pony. It was set in wooden splints and wrapped in bandages. He laid his head back and stared up at the boards that passed for a roof. This isn't what he expected hell to be like.

A couple of hours later, the Chinaman ducked in through the door and looked at him through squinted eyes. He quickly ducked back out. Not five minutes later, he came back in with a piece of old board and a stone. Titche watched as the Chinaman slid the board under his torso, lifted it, and slid the rock between the board and the cot. Titche was now in a reclined position, and the Chinaman was gone again just as quickly as before. The next time he came in, he was holding a bowl. He knelt beside the cot and dipped the spoon into its contents. He lifted a spoonful of broth and some rice and motioned for him to eat. Then he handed the bowl to Titche. There were a few small chunks of meat floating here and there, and something green in it. He figured it was a wild onion. He tasted it and it wasn't horrible. He ate and then set the bowl on the floor when he had finished.

Before long, the Chinaman popped back in. He picked up the bowl and smiled when he saw it was empty. He gave a small bow and disappeared back outside. When he came in next, he had a stout branch that had been carved into a makeshift crutch. He set it beside the cot and turned to go.

"Hey! Chinaman. Whiskey?" The Chinaman stared blankly. Titche made a show of pretending to hold a glass and drink. "Hooch?" The Chinaman disappeared. When he came back several minutes later, it was with a canteen. Titche unscrewed the cap hurriedly and put it to his lips thirstily. He thought it was his lucky day until water spilled into his mouth instead of whiskey. He pulled the canteen away quickly and started coughing from it going down the wrong pipe. He held it up. "This ain't what I asked fer!" The Chinaman took the canteen and disappeared. Titche waited and waited for him to pop back in, but the next time he came through the door was many hours later, at dusk. With him, he brought another bowl of broth. Titche knocked it from his hands, where it spilled onto the floor, where it slowly seeped into the dirt. The Chinaman seemed unperturbed and left again. An hour past dark, he came back. He had a bowl in one hand and a bandana with something in it in the other. He let one corner of the bandana go, and several of the little black stones rolled out to join the others in the corner. He set the bowl, full again of broth, next to the cot before going to the sleeping mat and lying down. He turned his back to Titche, and as far as he could tell, was asleep shortly afterwards.

During the night, wide awake, Titche picked up the bowl of broth. It was cold, but he didn't care. He was hungry.

When he woke up the next morning, it was because Mother Nature was calling in a big way. He reached for the makeshift crutch beside the cot and pulled it up. He swung around on the cot, putting his legs over the side and out straight. The board that had kept him reclined clattered to the floor. It took some doing, but he finally made it all the way up to standing. He hobbled out of the small shack, making sure not to hit his head on the door frame. Around the side of it, he watered a nearby tree like Mother Nature had requested.

He went back to the shack, but before going in, he looked around. It was a very small clearing on the side of a quick but small brook. Very large, tall trees surrounded the camp on all sides. There were a few younger ones trying to encroach around the edges. There was a much-used fire pit, several wooden bowls blackened on the inside and out, and a small wooden bench. In the stream, there were a few rock mounds. Titche's leg was starting to throb with pain. He ducked back into the shack and got back on the cot. He set the stone on the floor and lay down, pulling his injured leg up by the cloth of his jeans. Laid back out straight again, some of the throbbing disappeared.

He missed the drink so badly he thought it would drive him mad. The pain in his leg didn't help. Eating the same broth every day didn't help either. Although each day it did have more meat and the broth was getting thicker. Still, there was only so much of it a person could stand. Finally, one evening, the Chinaman came in with some roasted fish. Whether it really did or not, Titche thought it was about the best thing he had ever tasted!

For the next couple of weeks, Titche was a miserable patient. He cursed the Chinaman up and down. Snarled and growled about the food, the shack, and anything else he could think of. None of it seemed to offend the little man, though. He seemed to just keep on going about his daily business like he wasn't even there, but where and doing what, Titche could not figure out. Every so often, he brought in some more of the tiny black stones and added them to the pile. Titche figured he must have about twenty of them cluttering the corner. He just shook his head.

His leg had healed some. He was able to limp around without the crutches. His need for drink was fading, and he stopped being so burly, but depression started to sink in. His melancholy showed in his slumped shoulders, vacant gaze, and lack of interest or ambition.

Chapter 7: Recoveries
and Discoveries

It was before dawn at the end of the third week of his recovery, or maybe the start of the fourth week? The monotonous days were blending together in endless boredom, so it was hard to know for sure. Chinaman tugged on Titche's arm, bringing him wide awake. Blinking and rubbing his fists in his eyes, he sat up on the cot. "What is it?" He had decided at this point that China (as he now referred to him) didn't know any English. The little man motioned for Titche to follow him outside. Titche stood up, stretched, and ducked through the door into the fresh air. China put his hands on both of Titche's arms, turning him toward the rising sun. Then he stood next to him. He started stretching out his arms and moving them in slow half circles or circles, bending his wrists at ninety-degree angles. He also moved his feet and legs in a similar fashion, stretching them, bending them, creating circles and half-circles. Titche wondered if he was maybe going loco. China stopped and nudged his arm with his elbow. Then he made the same moves again. Titche got the idea that China wanted him to do the same. He turned to go back in. China was in front of him within seconds, blocking his way. He put his hand on Titche's chest where his heart was, and then he pointed to his head, "bad". Titche's eyes widened in surprise. He hadn't heard a word of English until now. China grabbed his arm and turned him toward the rising sun. "Work."

"China, I ain't gonna flail around like a fish in the grass." He turned to go back in again. China grabbed his arm and pulled him toward the little bench, patting it. Titche sat down with a grumble. Again, China touched his chest and his temple with his finger. "Bad. Work." He walked a few feet away and turned to the rising sun. For the next half hour or so, the little Chinaman moved his arms and legs to and fro and around in circles, bending and moving with a gracefulness that was actually captivating when you sat there and watched. As he watched, he couldn't decide if it looked more like a dance or a tree with its limbs swaying in the wind. When China was done, he gave the sun a small bow before he headed out of camp and into the deep shade under the massive trees.

Each morning after that was the same. China would wake him up and make him go outside. He wanted him to join his morning ritual. And if he refused, it was "bad work".

Titche gave in. He secretly admitted to himself that he had become rather curious about what China was doing. He stood next to him and tried to imitate his movements. He found out it was not as easy as it looked! He was tired long before the routine was over and found that his muscles were actually sore. China disappeared up the mountain, leaving Titche sitting on the bench. He massaged his aching muscles and thought about what that meant. He had gotten soft, he thought to himself, that's what it meant.

He had gone down a deep, dark hole on that fateful day that seemed so long ago, and now he was here, wherever that was. He had languished here, recuperating, and doing nothing to help out. He was eating what little food this man had. It was shameful, wallowing day in and day out, in his own misery like no one else but him had ever suffered a calamity. Plenty of others had. Maybe even China.

Yet this little man had not taken offense at his bad manners, had not sent him packing, shared what passed as a home with him, and fed him without complaint. He felt something he had not felt in a very long time: ambition. China was right. His heart and his mind had gone bad, poisoned by grief and alcohol. He needed to put himself to work and get himself right again, if that were possible. Each morning after that, Titche got up with China and went out to face the rising sun. He did his best to follow his lead through the ceremony each morning. Titche got stronger, and his movements smoother until, had anyone else been watching, they would have thought they both looked like tree branches bending and swaying and dancing in the wind.

It had only been a few weeks. Titche did the routine every morning with China and was finally keeping up with ease. His muscles no longer got sore, and he no longer limped when he walked. His leg was like new. While China was gone doing whatever it was he did all day, Titche had even started to do the routine again in the afternoon. It made him feel better, and it took away some of the boredom from the slowly passing days.

This morning, after they finished the exercises, China pointed at him and then touched his own heart and head. "Good." Titche smiled. China turned to go up the mountain but stopped and turned back around. He motioned for him to follow. "Work."

Titche understood and followed behind China. They disappeared into the forest, scrambling through the trees, and then climbed the mountainside higher and higher until there were fewer trees and many more boulders. China was headed toward one really large one. When they got to it and slipped around one side, Titche found himself looking into a rather large cave. China stepped in and lit a lantern he picked up from the floor. He pointed to a hefty metal rod that came to a point on one end and a small but bulky hammer. Titche picked them up and then proceeded to follow China as he led the way deep into the cave.

He made sure to stay close behind. They seemed to walk forever, following its twists and turns, deeper and deeper into the darkness, until Titche was feeling a little uncomfortable. He felt that he was somehow slowly being smothered by a hand he couldn't see or feel. The darkness was taking hold of him, and he was definitely getting anxious.

China turned into a smaller opening on the left. They hadn't walked too far when he turned and touched his arm. Then China held the lamp up to the wall. Titche couldn't believe what he was seeing. Gold. It was not a big vein of it, but it was there. China traded items with him and pulled Titche's arm up and close to the wall. Where the vein widened a little, China put the pointed end of the metal bar just off the edge of the gold and pounded on the other end with the mallet. It was hard work, and they took turns doing it. But after what seemed like several hours, they had managed to break free a few small chunks of gold. China put them in his pocket, picked up the lantern, and indicated it was time to go.

When they emerged from the cave, it was later than he would have expected. China blew out the lantern and set it down. He set down the hammer and metal spike next to it. Together they headed down the mountain, China's leading the way back to camp.

Once they got back, China started the fire in the fire pit. Titche figured he was starting dinner. Fish again, he thought, and cringed. It was the last thing he wanted to put in his mouth. Instead, China took a wooden bowl and filled it with water before setting it in the fire. He went to a nearby tree and scarred it with his knife. Sapped oozed out of the wound. He scraped it into a small wooden spoon that had a deep bowl, which he had pulled from his frock. Titche watched China do the same thing several more times. When the spoon was full of sap, China brought it to the fire. Most of the water had disappeared from the bowl in the form of steam, but China added the sap to the small amount that was left, stirring it and stirring it, until it was thick goop. He lifted the bowl off and added some crushed charcoal to it, stirring and stirring some more. When he was done, he had a thick black, sticky substance that would remind someone of tar. He reached into his pocket and pulled out the little gold nuggets from the cave. He dropped them into the substance and stirred them with the spoon. When they were thoroughly coated and the sap had started to harden up slightly, he took them out and set them on a rock to cool the rest of the way. It wasn't until then that China went to the stream and checked the fish traps.

Titche understood now. These were the little black stones China kept in the corner of the shack. If anyone happened along, no one would have a clue what they really were. This Chinaman was a very clever fellow! Titche had a whole new respect for him.

Every day after that was the same. Some days, they were not able to loosen any of the gold from the wall. Other days, they would get a few nuggets, adding them to the gradually growing pile in the corner.

Chapter 8: A trip to town

Titche figured he had been with China for three or four months when one morning, after the 'sunrise ceremony' as he now called it, China surprised him by going back in the shack instead of heading for the cave. He followed him in. China lifted his sleeping mat, and under it was a sack. He rolled it up and tucked it under his arm. He picked up two of the little black stones and handed them to him. He headed back out and turned to the west, jumping agilely across the stream, where he then headed southwest. Titche followed. It wasn't long, and they came to a faint and narrow trail. Titche was pretty sure this was the same trail little Bessie had met her demise on. China followed the trail south. They stayed at an easy pace for most of the day until they could hear the rushing water of a large river. They got a little closer before China turned off into the woods. They followed the sound of the water and came to the edge of the river. China led him to a very small fire ring and pointed. There was a small pile of firewood next to it already. Then China reached behind a nearby tree and pulled from it a wooden shaft with one end whittled to a point. He went to the river and jumped from stone to stone, getting away from the bank. As Titche got a fire started, he watched China throw the wooden stake into the water with more force than he would have thought he was capable of. Five throws netted two fish for dinner. After they had eaten, China searched in the woods and brought back another small pile of fire fuel that he put close by the small fire ring. He also had a piece of bark that he brought to the river and let soak. Titche sat by the very small fire, watching and wondering what China was going to do next. He pulled the bark from the river and set it in the fire before putting out his hand, palm up. It took Titche a minute, but then he realized China wanted the nuggets. He reached into his pocket, pulled them out, and dropped them into his palm. China dropped the nuggets onto the bark, which now had hot steam rising from it. In just a few short minutes, the hot steam had made the sap concoction melt off, leaving the two little gold nuggets exposed. He blew out the fire and lay down to sleep. Titche stayed awake a little longer, listening to the rush of the water and gazing at the bright stars peeping through the trees above before falling asleep himself.

Early the next morning, they were back on the path. Titche had the little nuggets in his pocket again. Within an hour, it ran into a much wider and more worn trail. China turned east onto it. Another hour of walking and they were on the outskirts of a surprisingly sizable town. Titche watched the hustle and bustle with new eyes and found himself rather fascinated by it all, like he was seeing it for the first time, even though he wasn't. Obviously, he had been in towns before now. The sound of horses and wagons, people talking and laughing, and the ring of metal being hammered on an anvil seemed very loud.

China led the way to a mercantile shop at the lower end of one of the busy streets. When they entered, a young man looked up from a paper he was reading spread on the goods counter. He smiled when he recognized China. "Wan!" he yelled. Within a minute, another Chinese man came into the room. He, too, smiled when he caught sight of China. He came over and gave him a short bow and then started speaking in his tongue. China smiled and spoke back at length, once turning to glance in Titche's direction. When he was done, the young Chinese man looked at Titche and said, "I am pleased to meet ch'ou. He says you are a son."

Titche's eyebrows raised up in surprise. "I'm pretty sure ya said that wrong. Anybody with eyes kin see I ain't his son."

"I am no wrong. He says ch'ou his son. To him, a son is someone who learn what their parents have to teach. They stay close and they work to help their parents when they age. Ch'ou have done these things. Ch'ou are his son."

Titche was speechless for a minute. "I don't even know his name. I call him China."

"No one know his name. I think it has passed from his memory. What is a name but a word? China is as good a word as any."

China spoke again in his own language, and the young man spoke back. Titche picked up the word China among the foreign words. He saw China chuckle at what the younger man said.

The younger man motioned them the rest of the way over to the goods counter. He got out a paper and something to mark with. China spoke again, and as he did, the young Chinese man made marks on the paper, the likes of which Titche had never seen before. He turned and looked at him. "Now, what would ch'ou like?"

"What would I like?"

"Yes. Ch'ou tell me what ch'ou would like and I go get it, no matter where in town. I bring things back here and ch'ou pay me."

"Oh. I have no money. No need fer ya ta get me anything."

"I mistake. I mean to say, China pays."

"Oh no, I couldn't let him do nothin' like that for me. He has already done more'n I can repay as it is."

The young Chinese man spoke rapidly. China stood straight, with a serious expression, listening. There was silence for a moment. Then China started to respond. The words were few with many breaks and said slowly. The young Chinese man flipped over the paper and started making more curious marks on the back. Several times, he looked at Titche, studying him closely. When China fell silent, 'young China' came around the counter with the marked-up paper clenched tightly in his fist. "I get these for ch'ou now and bring back. Ch'ou have something for me?" He held out his hand.

Titche stared at him. China pointed to his pocket. "Oh, right." He pulled the gold nuggets out of his pocket and put it in the other Chinaman's outstretched hand.

"Good. Now, follow me, please."

China walked with the young man, and Titche followed behind. They soon came to a wide building that resembled a barn but wasn't. There was a regular door and no windows. 'Young China' delivered three deliberate knocks followed by a light kick at the bottom of the door, and then it opened a crack. A young Chinese girl peered out. Her dark eyes took in the men standing patiently outside. 'Young China' spoke quickly to her, and she averted her eyes to the ground and opened the door wide enough for them to enter. China had apparently been here many times before and shuffled off into the gloom of the interior. 'Young China' asked, "Here ch'ou get bath, and shave, and haircut?"

"I told ya' I have no money."

"It is taken care of." 'Young China' spoke rapidly to the young Chinese girl, who flushed a little and glanced at Titche.

Titche noticed. "I'm not in need of any company, mister. I'm good." He didn't know how to go on. He was feeling a little awkward.

The young Chinese man chuckled. "No, this is not that kind of establishment. She is not the kind of worker. She is a little nervous because ch'ou are the first white man here. Only Chinese men come here. She is used to making baths, cutting hair, and things for Chinese. She is nervous? Uncertain? Shy. But she will do a good job. I leave

now. Many things to collect. I will be back." With that, he left on feet
that seemed to have grown wings all of a sudden.

The young woman looked up at Titche and gave a sincere and
brave smile. He responded in kind, and she made a motion for him to
follow. They passed many shut doors, eventually coming to one that
was open. Inside was a small room with a fire pit, a bucket, stones
here and there on the floor, a washtub, a chair with a couple of towels
draped over the back, and a small table holding a mirror, straight razor,
lye soap, and scissors.

Titche watched the girl as she started the fire going in the pit and
tapped his chest, saying, "Titche". She understood immediately and
put her hand gently on her own chest and said, "Su-Lei". He smiled
and nodded. With the fire going now, she put the stones in it, and then
proceeded to the tub where she worked a hand pump and filled it about
half full of water. Su-Lei said something in Chinese.

Titche stared at her and shrugged.

She looked at the water in the tub and back at him. Then she put
her hand in it and made a cold, shivering kind of motion for a second.
She took her hand out but put it right back in and yanked it out fast
and fanned herself like she was hot.

Titche got the idea and fanned himself.

Su-Lei smiled. Grabbing a towel from the back of the chair, she
picked out the stones from the fire, which were now very hot, and put
them in the bath. She felt the water and repeated this task until she
was satisfied with the temperature of the bath. Then she took the
stones out and rolled them across the floor. She walked to Titche and
gave a gentle tug on his shirt and trousers and pointed to the chair.
Grabbing the soap from the little table, she put it next to the tub and
then disappeared out the door, shutting it softly behind her.

It didn't take him long to strip down and step into the tub. It was just right. Su-Lei had done an excellent job. He lowered himself into the hot water and got comfortable. Reaching for the soap, he lathered up from head to foot before dropping it outside the tub and then submerging himself. He came up sputtering, wiping water from his eyes, nose, and mouth. Then he leaned back and relaxed. Titche wasn't sure how long he had been there when there was a light tap. Su-Lei stuck her head around the door slowly so as to give him a chance to cover up if he needed to before stepping the rest of the way in and looking up. She made the shiver and the hot sign again. Titche understood and shook his head no and put up his hands, palms out, in a stop motion. He pointed to his clothes on the chair. Su-Lei smiled and nodded, then left again.

Titche climbed regretfully out of the tub and got dressed. He put the chair next to the tub, sat down, and with a mirror in hand, used the tub water to shave with. Su-Lei was back quickly. With a light tap, she entered the room as before, slowly, with her head down, and then looked up. Seeing him shaving, she made scissor movements with her fingers. Titche nodded. She picked up the scissors from the small table and started trimming his wild tangle of dark curls. When they were both done, he stood up and put his hands out, palm up in a gesture of "well?". Su-Lei looked him over, smiled, and blushed. She gave him a nod of approval before she scurried out the door.

Titche followed her out and found China and 'young China' near the front door talking in their native language. China looked him up and down and gave a nod of approval.

"Ch'ou looks well. Respectable. Come. I have many packages."

Back at the mercantile, 'young China' picked up two large sacks. He handed one to China and the other to Titche. The sacks had a long strap running from the top to the bottom. He watched China put his head and one arm through. The sack was against his back, and the strap ran diagonally across his chest. Titche did the same. It was surprisingly comfortable. Then 'young China' handed them each a long wooden staff. Last, he handed them a package wrapped in brown paper and tied with a string. "Safe travels." He gave a short bow.

"I don't need a walkin' stick." He held it out.

"That is not a walking stick."

China said something in Chinese, and 'young China' responded. With another set of bows, China turned for the door, and they headed for home.

They stopped. The same place they had last night, even though it was not far from town. China motioned to Titche to open the package, then started opening his. Inside was a sizable meal complete with noodles, rice, vegetables, bread, braised meat, and some cookies he had never seen before. Titche's stomach growled. China heard and chuckled. It had been a very long time since Titche had a real meal, even before he met China. He thought about the broth with the meat. He didn't like to think about it, but he had a suspicion it was poor old Bessie. Since then, they had been eating fish. He dug in, shamelessly, shoveling food in his mouth. He had never eaten Chinese food before, and it definitely tasted much different from what he was raised on, but boy, was it good! By the time he was done, he was as full as a wood tick.

China had only eaten half his and wrapped the rest back up before stretching out on the ground with his eyes shut. Titche couldn't tell if he was asleep or just relaxing. He stretched out, too, and pulled his hat over his eyes. Listening to the birds and the water, with a full belly, on a beautiful day, was like a little piece of heaven. He thought of Annabelle and wondered if this was how she was living in heaven. If so, that isn't so bad, I guess, he thought to himself.

Chapter 9: New Lessons

The rest of the trip back to camp was uneventful. The sack was feeling pretty heavy for the last leg of the journey, so they took a few extra rest stops. Once back, they unpacked. There were food supplies (thankfully), several packages of seeds, two blankets, and clothes. Titche realized the seeds were for a small garden. He also realized, for the first time, that China had ripped up the only blanket he had and used it as bandages for his leg when he first brought Titche back to his camp, and that realization was humbling. As for the clothes, China had apparently instructed 'young China' to get two pairs of denims and two new shirts for Titche, and he had done a good job because they were the right size for the most part. Last, Titche pulled a pair of high moccasins out of the bag. He held the soft doeskins in his hands and stared at them, puzzled. They had fine fringe and beadwork as well.

China could see that he was puzzled. He came over and tapped the cowboy boots he was wearing with his hand. "Bad." He looked at Titche and did it again. "Bad." He was frowning. He took the moccasins from Titche and felt them with his hands. "Good." He smiled. Titche did not look convinced. China pointed to his boots again and then covered his ears and shook his head. He held up the moccasins and then cupped his ear and leaned forward like he was listening.

Titche got what he was saying. Walking to the cave in boots made noise that someone could hear. Walking in moccasins made much less noise. He had never worn them, and he did not like the thought, but

China had done so much for him that if he wanted him to give the moccasins a go, he would.

The next morning, Titche put on the moccasins and walked around. It was definitely different, but they were a lot more comfortable than he had expected. China had gone outside already. Titche went to join him to do the 'sunrise ceremony.' But this morning, China was holding the walking sticks that weren't really walking sticks according to 'young China'. China handed him one. Then he swung it here and there, flipping it, while moving around. He had moved so fast that it surprised Titche. It also surprised him that the walking stick didn't seem cumbersome at all in his hands. China stood straight facing Titche and held the stick in one hand in front of him, waiting. Titche got the message and imitated him. China went through the moves again, very slowly this time, so Titche could follow along. This became the new morning routine. Within a couple of weeks, Titche could wield the 'walking stick' as he still called it, as easily and masterfully as China.

Chapter 10: Farewell Fairview Valley

Titche's eyes opened, and visions of a small idyllic camp far from where he was now faded away. It was replaced with the grainy light of pre-dawn, where everything is colored in shades of gray. He lay still in the bed and just listened. Everything was quiet. It wasn't long, and the first bird of the morning started singing its praise. Soon, others were joining in.

He got up and stretched. After getting dressed and pulling on his moccasins, he stood, and even though the room was small, went through the motions China had taught him years ago. They still made him feel better somehow. More centered.

Going out his private door and down the back stairs, he wondered if Clap was up and at the stable yet. He didn't have to wonder long. It was a short walk, and as he approached the barn, he saw the doors were already open.

Inside, Titche could see fresh hay in the stalls and fresh water already. Clap was in one of the stalls, shoveling up the manure. His three horses, plus another one, were out in the corral kicking up their heels.

"Good morning, Clap."

Clap turned around, startled. "Good morning, Mr. Titche. You're sure up early! Not many get up at the crack of dawn."

He smiled. "No, they sure don't. I thought I'd saddle up an' ride out ta those ranches this morning an' look over their horses iff'n they don't mind unexpected visitors."

Clap leaned on his shovel. "No, no, they're real good people an' as hospitable as ya could ask fer. I think you'll see they take good care of their stock, Mr. Titche. Those horses of ur'n will have a likely place ta live and work."

"Good. How do I find 'em?"

"Just go right out straight from the stable and across the little creek. Turn left and follow it'a spell. You'll come to a trail. Take it to the right. That trail will form a Y a coup'la miles out. The left goes to the T Double Box and the right goes to the M Bar M."

"Which one should I go ta first? Think on it hard. Which one would make a better home? Where they'd get some pamperin'?"

Clap rubbed his whiskered chin and looked thoughtful. "Well, they's both good places, but I guess I'd go on out ta the T Double Box first. They have more horses there an I'd say, because of that, each one has less work and more grazen' time."

Titche touched his hat brim. "Thanks, Clap. I'll do that."

Titche caught Broken and brought him into the barn. He brushed him with the little brush out of the saddlebag for about fifteen minutes before saddling him and heading out. Clap was impressed all over again by how much time this cowboy took with his horse. It was uncommon.

After Titche found the trail Clap had told him about, he let Broken decide the pace. Broken's decision was a distance-consuming lope until he was winded and wound it down to a walk. By that time they had covered so much ground that they were already on the T Double Box spread. A split rail fence came into view around a large pasture

54

that boasted tall waves of grass blowing gently in the breeze. Watching the grass fold over on itself and then fold back over in the opposite direction, like ripples washing ashore in a lake, was mesmerizing. Titche pulled up and just watched until Broken started fidgeting, letting him know he was ready to move on. Following the wagon path along the fence, Titche glanced frequently out into the pasture. There were quite a few horses grazing on the grass, tails swooshing back and forth to ward off flies. They were beautiful, healthy animals that were well taken care of.

They were coming to the end of the split rail fence, where it hooked to a corral. The corral, in turn, was hooked to one side of a very large barn. The bunkhouse was not far from it, and on the left was a ranch house. A tall, older gentleman had come out onto the veranda. A cowboy putting a new shoe on a zebra dun finished what he was doing and stood holding the horse's lead rope, watching him ride into the yard. Another cowboy came from the darkness of the interior of the barn to lean against the door frame.

Titche pulled Broken to a stop about ten feet from the cowboy and the horse. "Howdy." He touched the brim of his hat with his finger. The rancher came down off the porch and strode towards them, stopping next to the same cowboy who had just said Howdy back.

Titche nodded to the older gentleman. "You must be the ranch owner? My name is Titche."

"I am Sam Cully. What can we do for you, Titche?"

"I've been wanderin' some. I came across a gruesome sight a couple'a day's ride west of that town back yonder. A young cowboy was tortured and murdered. It weren't the first time on my travels I had seen such. I thought I would ride out here and warn ya that there's an outlaw bunch in the neighborhood. One of 'em rides a beautiful black and white Paint with an X branded on the hind quarter, I'm told.

They seem ta target isolated ranches, or cowboys alone an' nowhere in patic'lar. I got ur name from a fella named Clap. I didn't mention it to none of 'em in town about the bunch 'cause they seem to mind themselves when they hit a town. No need to stir up trouble *there* and get folks killed."

The cowboy from the barn had had enough of holding up the door frame, so he walked over to join the group and heard what Titche said about the murder. His eyes got big, and he looked at Sam Cully. "Boss, ya don't suppose that'd be JW?"

Sam looked worried. "Can you describe the dead cowboy?"

"Well, I'd say young. Five and a half feet or so. Dirty blond hair. A long scar ran from his wrist to his elbow on the inside of one arm."

"That's JW, boss! Remember that mean ole mossy horned bull hooked him good that time out in the North pasture? He had so many stitches, I couldn't even count 'em all!"

"It does sound like him. Can you describe his horse?"

"Weren't no horse anywhere nor anything but his blanket still spread on the ground."

The other cowboy piped up. "We need to get some boys rounded up and go after these murderin' polecats an' string 'em high!"

Titche could see he was boiling over angry! "Ya don't have ta worry about that. I've been trailin' this bunch fer some time now. They're an evil yer mamma never warned ya 'bout. I got one of 'em last month when his horse went lame from a broken shoe an' he fell behind. I got two more of 'em shortly after they killed your pard when they came a'checkin' their back trail. I won't stop trailin' the stinkin' coyotes until I get 'em all boots up."

Sam nodded his head in agreement. "I take it you've got cards in this game, Titche."

"My parents, my wife, newborn son, and a horse ranch."

Sam's expression turned grim. "I'm really sorry to hear that." The other two cowboys shook their heads in agreement. "That is a mighty fine horse you've got there. Is he one from your ranch?"

"No, I got lucky an' picked him up along the way. As fine an animal as I ever had, though."

The angry cowboy spoke up again. "Wait until JW's brother hears. It won't be good fer those outlaws. If yer on their trail, we should just get the hands together an' go after 'em. How many are there? How far behind are ya?"

"I'd say there's about ten left, maybe? I don't rightly know how far behind I am. After killing the last two, I backtracked and headed this way. I was going to try to cut their trail up ahead somewhere."

"That makes no sense! You should'a stuck to their trail! Why'd you come this way fer? They'll get away, sure as the south grows cotton!"

Sam interjected. "No, Pitch. That's actually quite smart. They'll be wastin' time trying to gully wash him, and instead, Titche will be ahead of 'em and that'll give him the upper hand."

"That's kinda my thoughts on it. That, an' I'm one man against ten. I want to make sure I keep pulling air long enough to ventilate each one of the low-down snakes. An' like I said, this bunch is an evil I have never seen nor heard of in my life time or my Pa's."

"Can you tell us what happened to JW?"

"I could Mr. Cully but I won't. It's not somethin' fittin' for any decent feller ta see or hear tell of. I buried him the best I could. His grave is in a little clearin' on not far from the Y in the trail. What was yer puncher doin' so far from the ranch, alone?"

"We appreciate you doing that for him. He was a good kid. He was headed for Wells Deep. He was carrying a substantial amount of cash and was going to bring back a new wagon. Ours is worn out. We've had to repair the repairs. That, some horses to pull the wagon, and some supplies for the ranch. Now, I wish I would have waited instead of sending him, but he was keen ongoing. Said there was someone gonna be there he hadn't seen in a month of Sundays. His brother, I would guess."

"Yeah. I've been there. These outlaws may not be headed there yet but, Paradise seems ta be the hub ta their spokes. Somehow, they keep circling back to it. They may circle around this way though. Since I been trailin' em', I've discovered they're a wiley bunch. Ya think there headed a certain way or ta certain place, but all of a sudden like, they turn an' do a loop aroun', comin' back on their own trail an' foller'n it. Then they may keep goin' on ta the next town or they may make another loop. One place ya *don't* want to be is on their back trail iffn' they've made a loop. In towns, they have themselves a time of it but not so's much as will attract the law. Which brings me back to my ride out this'a'way. Since I don't know if they're getting ready ta do a loop, you an' yer neighbors need to keep a sharp eye out an' be ready."

"Neighbor. There are only two ranches in this part of the country. It's too isolated for most folks."

"Would ya like me to ride on ta the other ranch an' let 'em know ta be on the watch?"

"No, thanks. I'll send Jake over. He's sparkin' a filly named Alice. He uses any excuse he can find to ride over." Sam grinned at the cowboy holding the lead of the horse. Jake blushed.

"That'll work. Before I head back, I brought two horses int'a town with me. They were the rides fer those two outlaws that I liberated from their evil ways. They aren't the quality ya have here, but they're good horses an' in need of a good home. I know some folks are superstitious about taking a dead man's horse. Do ya think you or your neighbor would be interested?"

"Either of us would. We don't get any horse peddlers this way, and horses age out. How much are you asking?"

"Fer you, nothin'. I look at it like yer owed them horses an' more. Those men killed one of yer own. An' I see they'd be well takin' care of here. They've earned it after bein' on the owl hoot trail fer so long. They're paid up fer at the stable in town 'til Friday. Could a couple of boys pick 'em up then?"

"Sure, they go wash the dust off and out every Friday and Saturday, anyway."

"Keep in mind, ya damn sure don't want ta be caught unawares an' lightly armed. I'd keep 'em bunched an' guards out. Also, I'd appreciate any talk of me didn't leave this yard. These hombres don't know what I look like. I'd like to keep it that'a'way."

"No, Titche, I agree with that. We won't be caught unawares or under-armed if we can help it at all. I'm gonna send Pitch, here, out to gather up the boys and Jake, here, with him. Once they have told all the boys to come back to the bunkhouse, the two of them can ride together to the M Bar M. Maybe even three of the boys together. I'll let them figure it out." Sam turned to them and said, "You boys understand? It wouldn't hurt for three of you to ride over, even if one of the others can go. And don't be running your mouths too much either. We need to give Titche all the advantage he can get. If they ask at the M Bar M, you just tell them the boss found out somehow and leave it like that. If that bunch of outlaws shows up here, we will dish out some of our own justice for our good friend and a good hand, JW."

"Yes, boss." They turned in unison and headed for the barn.

Titche and Sam shook hands, and then Titche turned and headed back to town.

Once back at the stable, he made it a point to check his own horse's shoes. All of them were snug and in excellent shape. He brushed Broken out and then released him into the corral with the others. Clap joined him at the corral. "How'd it go at the T Double Box?"

"Good, Clap. Sam's boys will be in town Friday night and bring these two back with them Saturday morning. Ya were right, they will be well taken care of there. They have plenty of pasture."

"I knew ya would approve! Ya missed Mable's dinner bell." Clap looked pretty put out by that. "But, I got ya a plate, an' I hope ya don't mind, but I left it in ur room. Even cold, her dinner shouldn't be discounted!"

Titche smiled and clapped him on the shoulder. "Thanks, pard. Appreciate it! Do I owe you the dollar or Miss Mable?"

Clap beamed at the compliment. "Me. Whenever yer ready, no rush."

Titche dug in his pocket and got out a dollar. "Here ya are, Clap. I'm gonna go fill my belly full." He started to walk away but stopped and turned around. "Clap?" He looked up from shaking out new hay in the stalls. "I need to ask you a favor."

"Well, sure, Mr. Titche."

"If anyone comes a'askin' about me, the less said the better. The outlaws I put six feet under. They had friends. Right now, they don't know nothin' about me. Not the color of my horse or how tall I stand in my socks. An', if that bunch comes here, ya keep yer head down an' mind yer business best ya can. They're pizen mean."

Clap looked very solemn. "You got it, Titche. I'll reign in my memory."

On that note, Titche turned back around. A few minutes later, he was climbing the back stairs to his room. Inside, he sat on the bed and lifted the towel off the plate of food. Green beans, two corn on the cob, mashed potatoes, roast beef piled high and doused in gravy, half loaf of homemade bread, and a thick slice of raspberry pie. It was a meal fit for a king. Mable was not just a good cook; she was exceptional. Maybe someday, under better circumstances, he would come back here for a while. Titche sprawled out on the bed. It was early in the day, but he wanted to get to sleep. He wanted to leave in the dark of night so no one would know which way he headed.

When he woke up, it was dark and quiet except for an owl somewhere who seemed to be having an argument with another owl of a different breed. The two hoots were distinguishably different. He got out of bed and dressed. Back to cold camps, he thought. With some disappointment, he gathered his belongings and headed for the stable.

Broken nickered when he came in. In a short time, he was saddled and headed out of town. He decided to go north. That was where the outlaws were headed. Paradise seemed to be the center of their territory. If they did loop around in this direction, Titche was going to try to be on high ground. He wanted to try to lay eyes on them from a safe distance.

Chapter 11: Paradise

As he rode, he thought about Paradise. It was a fair-sized town of mixed nationalities, so anything you wanted, you could get. That was where China brought him after he had recuperated. They had made a total of four visits to that town in the short time they were together. The fifth visit, Titche was alone.

He had awakened one morning, and China was still asleep, back to him, on his sleeping mat. Except he wasn't asleep. China had crossed the great divide during the night, peacefully. Titche was deeply saddened at his loss. He found a beautiful spot close to the cabin and the creek and made China his forever home. He put the sleeping mat in the bottom and rolled him in his blanket. Next to him, he laid the 'walking stick' and a small black stone. After he filled it in, he piled it high with stones from the brook. He would sleep forever in complete safety. Nothing would ever be able to disturb him.

He had stayed about two weeks, trying to work the mine alone and carry on with the daily routines, but he found his mind wandering back in time to his beautiful wife and baby boy and the ranch he had loved. A thought started to take shape in his mind. There was nothing holding him here but grief. It was time to step out into the world. No expectations, just see what happens. After all, he had none when he ended up here in this camp with China.

He collected what food would last on the road, his blanket, and his 'walking stick'. He also collected all the little black stones from the corner of the camp. Then he headed to Paradise.

The first person he went to see was 'young China'. Wan, which was his given name, was really the only person he knew except Su-Lei. He informed him of China leaving this world and heading for the pearly gates of eternity.

Wan shook his head sadly. "At least, in the end, there was you, Titche. You gave him honor, and this is important to us Chinese."

"Well, does he have family somewhere? I thought maybe I could deposit his assets in a bank account for them here in Paradise."

Wan looked startled and concerned. "No, he has no family. What was his is now yours. He would want that. You do not want to deposit anything in this bank, I think."

"Why would that be?"

"There is something. I dunno. Many banks being robbed in other towns. This bank was never robbed. A man come here sometimes with fat saddlebags. When he comes, he goes to the bank and not come out for a long while. This man has hard, soulless eyes. I have seen him close, twice. I leave the bank, he comes in as I go. He and Banker seem very close. I think banker tell him things. I think his bank no robbed because of it. I think you deposit gold there and he will tell that man. I think he will kill you in the night, or worse, when you least expect it."

Titche sighed. "I need a coupl'a things, Wan. I need a matchin' pair of colts complete with holsters, lots of bullets, a riffle with lots of loads for that too, matching Bowie knives sharp enough to shave with that'll fit in the top of my moccasins, hard tack for the road, some grain, two canteens, a long duster, saddle, saddlebags, bridle, rope, lead rope, and saddle blanket. While you're getting that together, I'm going to visit the stables and look at some horses. When I find one I like, I'll have you go get that too." Titche took out two small black stones and handed them to Wan, who looked at them curiously.

"Sorry, Wan, they are covered in pitch and charcoal to disguise the nuggets. If ya steam them, the pitch will run right off."

Wan's eyebrows raised, and the corners of his mouth turned up in almost a smile. He rolled the nuggets around in his palm. "Clever. Clever." Then he disappeared.

Titche walked around the stables in town looking for a good horse. All the ones he had seen so far were mediocre at best. The third stable he came to, he leaned on the rail, looking at the horses in the corral. One horse's head shot up, and he stared back at Titche like he was sizing him up. Titche liked how alert and brazen he was. He was big, muscular, and observant of all that was happening around him. And, he seemed to have 'horse sense,' which is really to say that if he was a person, he would be able to reason. He could tell that the horse just knew somehow that he was being evaluated and judged. The horse walked with a purposeful stride over to Titche, but not quite close enough for him to reach out and touch. Getting a closer look, Titche could see quite a few scars. Some were from horse fights, and a few looked like bullet grazes. He was in bad need of brushing, and his hooves were in bad need of grooming. But the horse looked sound, and he seemed highly intelligent.

A hostler magically appeared next to Titche. He realized he must have been standing there for quite some time. "Sum'thin' I could help' ya with, mister?"

Titche pointed to the horse staring back at him just inches out of his reach. "Does someone own this horse?"

The hostler chewed his tobacco for a minute and then spit a long brown stream out of the side of his mouth and into the dirt. "Well, as a matter of fact, not no more." He chuckled, and it was not a pleasant sound. "I jus' bought that one from a man who said his pard'ner wouldn't be a'needing it anymore, iffn' ya understand me. He had no use fer him. Said the hoss was broken, notional, couldn't trust him to do what ya told him ta do and gets worse ev'r time ya whip him or spur him."

"An outlaw's horse, then?"

"Well, now, I'm not one to judge a man. I just buy, sell, an' take care of hosses fer some's that come ta town." He paused. When Titche didn't say any more, he continued on. "I can't say as the gent who sold him was an outlaw or not. He was a fine-looking man, with expensive tastes. Why, jus' the rig on his hoss was more'n I'm likely ta see in a year. And that hoss was a beaute! Finest Paint I ever did see!"

"With an X brand on its rump."

The hostler looked at Titche with suspicion. "How'd ya know that?"

"I didn't." Titche turned and left. The hostler stared after him.

Back at the Wan's Mercantile, Wan had all of the requested items laid out for Titche to look over. He nodded his approval. "Iffn' I can't put this gold in the bank, I'm not sure what I should do with it. I don't want it takin' up room in my saddlebags. Some of it needs to be turned into double eagles. I can't go around spending gold nuggets. I'll have every outlaw in a hundred miles after me. An' I found a horse, Wan. Is there enough left over?"

"Plenty. Can I see the nuggets?" Titche pulled them out of the sack. "Will you trust Wan? I think I have an answer for your problem."

"You've always been a good man before. No need fer me ta doubt ya now."

"I take care of it." Wan scooped up the little black stones and was gone quicker than a lizard catching a fly. Titche went out and down the street for what would be the last hot bath he would have for a while.

When Titche got back, He found the horse in front of the mercantile, saddled and ready to go. He went in to see Wan. "I got you a new hat." He handed a new black Stetson to Titche, who looked it over curiously because he had not asked for a new hat. That's when he noticed the band around the crown. Evenly spaced and sewn to it were little black stones!

"Look closely inside."

Titche looked at the inside. Evenly spaced were little pockets of silk, each one held a double eagle that could be pushed out through the side.

Wan handed him his duster. The buttons from the front had been replaced with little black stones. There was a pocket on the left breast of it. Now it had another secret pocket inside, which also held several double eagles. Inside the duster on the right, another pocket had been sewn in, just like the one on the outside. Titche smiled.

"You will find bridle and saddle have the same matching trim as hat band and duster buttons."

"That is truly amazin', Wan. I surely appreciate this."

"My pleasure. Don't be a stranger. Go, but come back."

They shook hands, and Titche mounted up. He didn't know where to look for this outlaw, but he had nothing but time.

Chapter 12: Outlaws

"Big T, Riff and Trey should'a been back by now."

The campfire burned high. The boys were coming down from the blood craze caused by torturing the unlucky cowpoke they had found along the trail. The adrenaline always brought it on. It took a couple of nights in camp to get them settled enough for him to control again before they could move on. The more victims, the longer it took to get them back down off their high. Being the leader of one of the most vicious outlaw bunches the Northwest had ever seen was not for fools or those who were not absolutely fearless and without compassion. He didn't respond, just stared into the fire.

Jules' horse went lame, and they never saw him again. It was odd, Jules never showed any sign of wanting to quit the bunch, but he could let it go. There could be any number of reasons he never showed up in Bluxy. Riff, on the other hand, could not let it go. Once he got a bur under his saddle, he wouldn't stop bucking until you got it out and held it in your hand for him to see. He took a notion in his head that something had happened to Jules. Someone had killed him. And once he got that notion, he got the notion there was someone on their backtrail, stalking them, like a cougar soundlessly stalking a hapless fawn. He kept going on about how he got the spider feelings on the back of his neck.

The day they killed that cow-nurse, that night at the campfire, Riff wasn't even wound up about it. He was sullen and surly. With the rest of the bunch running high spirits, celebrating, Big T couldn't have Riff acting that way or something bad was likely to go down right in camp. Riff was bound to say something to the wrong person at the wrong time and a fight would brew. Men would choose sides and it would be a catastrophe. Whoever wasn't dead in the end would never be able to work with each other again thanks to hard feelings and grudges. He told Riff that if he felt that way in the morning, he could go check the back trail. They would need a couple of nights in camp for the men to come back down to earth anyway and it would get Riff out of camp so he couldn't stir up more trouble being surly. Plus, once Riff found out no one was back there, he could shoot this stalking notion in the head and put it to rest once and for all. Riff had stalked off to bed but was at least content.

Now he was gone. And not only him, but Trey also, who had insisted on going with him. They had left camp yesterday morning and should have been back last night. Big T had given them another day to return, wondering if they had found someone trailing them after all, and maybe it had taken some time for them to take care of the problem, or maybe they had *taken time* to take care of the problem. A cruel smile formed on his lips. But now it was late in the evening on day two, and they were still not back. The unconscious smile that had formed a minute ago faded away.

Big T had to think. Those two didn't quit the bunch. That was a fact. Past that, he could only surmise. As unlikely as it seemed to be, he now believed someone was back there. Once could be chance. Twice? Only a fool would believe that.

So, who could it be? It was not the law. Big T and his bunch had robbed a few banks, some stages, some miners, strangers along the trail, and some remote ranches. But they never left a single witness behind. Even if their loved ones were trying to track down the outlaws responsible, they would have *nothing at all* to go on. Besides, even if they somehow did, they would get together a little posse and come on, hell bent for justice.

For the first time ever, Big T was stumped, and he couldn't let these desperados get wind of it.

Jules had disappeared months ago. Someone following them with vengeance on their mind wouldn't be taking this long to try to pick them off. Big T stared into the fire, trying to find a logical answer. If he knew the problem, he could find a solution.

It was quiet. Too quiet. Big T looked around the fire. All eyes were on him and no one was making a sound. All eyes were on him and no one was making a sound. He had it to do, and he had to do it now.

"Somehow we got trouble trailin' us. Riff was right all along, that crazy bastard. We all go back down the trail tomorrow. No one wanders off. Ya gotta piss, take someone with ya. Now, get some sleep. I want you boys ta be alert tomorrow, like we're pulling a job." He stayed by the fire and watched the other outlaws disappear one by one. That little speech had definitely sobered them up. He had no doubt they would be ready to ride in the morning.

During the night, it rained, a soft shower that only lasted a couple of hours.

Chapter 13: Back and Forth

The next morning, the outlaws were up, drying out around the campfire, and drinking copious amounts of coffee. They were a solemn and focused lot. Big T was no one to mess with. These outlaws that rode with him now knew it to be a fact. They had seen him personally kill several of their members in the past for small lapses in judgement. There was a Mex, once, that made the mistake of hiding some hooch in his saddlebags. Whiskey was strictly prohibited on the trail. When Big T caught him nipping at it, he put a blade in the small of his back, right between two vertebrae. The Mex went down like a rag doll. His legs didn't work anymore. Big T dragged him to a tree and strung him up by the hands. Then Big T very carefully cut along his abdomen and let his intestines spill out. That Mex was screaming like something none of them had ever heard before. Big T took his bandana from around his neck and shoved it in his mouth. There they left him, just like that. Another one, a young outlaw just starting down the owl hoot trail, made the mistake of lying to him. Big T put a gun to his head and had him strip before tying him up. After that, he found a rotten log and rolled it over. Ants welled out of the ground. He pinned the kid down where the log was, stuck a stick in the kid's mouth so he couldn't shut it, and then poured some honey from the bottle he kept in his saddlebag down the kid's throat. The idea was that the ants would eat him from the inside out. He cut his eyelids off, too, just because he could. It made the rest of the bunch uncomfortable when they filed past the kid and left him there. No one crossed Big T.

He mounted up and the rest of the outlaws mounted up behind him. They started back down the trail they had just come up a few days earlier. Big T expected to find his men somewhere along the trail, even dead, though no one had heard any gunshots. But he knew from experience that there were plenty of other ways to kill a man than shoot him. As they rode, the outlaws had their heads on swivels, and no one spoke.

When they got to the spot where they had tortured the cow-nurse, they saw he was cut down and buried. There was no sign to be had because of the rain from the night before. They continued down the trail to where a second trail cut off from it. Still, they had found no bodies and no signs of their pards' horses.

Big T sat his horse in thought. He didn't like it. Whoever this was, he was like a ghost. Now he had another decision to make, and one he liked even less. He would have to split the bunch. It was bad business. Keeping them together at all times kept them unified, and no one got any ideas, with him right there to remind them that they don't have any.

His other option was to turn around again and carry on with their original plan to go to Paradise. He had to make a deposit at the bank and find out if the banker had any news for him. The boys would be out of money again by the time they were ready to leave town. Sometimes they reminded him of cattle- eat, drink, shit, and go where you tell them to. Nothing more to them except they were riled and rowdy. They had no plans for when the day would come that they couldn't outlaw anymore. After all, all good things come to an end, eventually.

He had a plan. Most of his take went into the bank. When he had played all his cards and was finally ready to call, that bank would be the last one he ever robbed. He would withdraw all his money and everyone else's, too. And that smug banker, who thought he was calling all the shots? He would be riding out of town in front of him with a colt pointed at his back. When they were safely away from civilization, he was going to show him who *really* called all the shots and just how uncivilized he could be.

Big T came out of his musing. All his men were sitting their horses, quietly waiting for his next command. Inside he was jelly. Never had he not been able to solve a problem quickly and with finality. He felt an intense hatred for this man, whoever he was, for putting him in this position for the first time in his life.

He leaned on his saddle horn and scrutinized his men. "If he was riding trail an' happened on that cow-nurse an' then went back to that town an' told the sheriff, we certainly would have run into a posse by now. Since we know he didn't go back an' tell the sheriff, that could only mean he is riding the vengeance trail. How that would be, I can't imagine. So, we either missed him along this trail or he has gone up that other trail." Big T nodded toward it. "I can't figure why he would kill two of us and then back off, iffn' it's vengeance he's after. Either we split up or we ride together to Paradise. I'm inclined to ride together to Paradise. But I don't like having a shadow." Big T was quiet again. "I think we will split up. DON'T make me regret this decision. Ya know how I can get when I don't get my way." He looked hard at his men, many of whom squirmed in their saddles. "I want you four to head up that trail and swing around toward Elk Canyon. We will meet at the cabin there. Hopefully, one or ta'other of us will have good news. From there, we ride to Paradise, and we won't be waitin' around or coming to find ya. Be there. We'll give it two weeks and see if we can smoke this gent out. Ride slow an' careful, an' keep an eagle eye out. Us splitting up should make him worry. Hopefully, he will make a mistake. The rules remain even though I am not there. No drinking, no whoring, no trouble. Let me find out otherwise, and I will make sure yer educated on the errors of yer ways before ya meet yer maker." Every man in the bunch nodded. They knew he spoke the truth. "Stick together, men. Like I said before, ya gotta piss, take someone with ya. I don't want to lose any more men." With that, the group split.

Chapter 14: Split and Play the Odds

Utah was part savage and part white, but he looked more savage. Abandoned as a young child, neither race wanting to accept him, he grew up stealing and fighting to survive. He hadn't expected to make it past thirty, but he made that milestone last year. He had never known any mercy, so he felt no mercy. This life was all he knew.

Whiskers was a slight, short, unassuming man of about fifty; the type you would walk past and never notice. He had no talent at all for anything except being overlooked. To Big T, he was essential for gathering up information.

Quinn was young, early twenties, and had the reflexes of a cat. He could stick to a bronco like butter on a chunk of bread. It didn't matter how much of a man-killer the horse was. No amount of kicking and rearing was going to knock Quinn off where it could stomp his guts into the dirt. He was also crazy fast and accurate with a pistol. He could draw and kill a man so quick that he would never know how he died, just that he did. If it involved speed, Quinn was the man you were looking for. Other than that, no one knew anything about him. He never talked much.

Last in the group of four was Griz, which was short for Grizzly. They called him that because he was a big man who was slow to anger. But once you crossed the line, he was like a big boar with porcupine quills in his mouth. He would smash anything within reach, and once he got his hands on you, he was going to tear you limb from limb or squeeze you until every bone in your body was broken.

The four of them rode the trail slowly, headed Northeast. Griz and Whiskers were looking for any sign that the rain hadn't washed out the night before, while Utah and Quinn kept their eyes peeled for any movement among the trees or on the cliff ledges further away. It was an uneventful couple of days.

The trail ended at another trail that had seen some wagon use. The choice was North or South. They headed north since Elk Canyon was in that direction. By midafternoon, they were looking at a small town in a wide valley between mountain ranges. They stopped. Each of them was inspecting the small arrangement of buildings.

Quinn sidled up to Utah. "What do ya think, Utah?"

"It sure ain't much o'nothin'. But there's a stable an' a saloon..."

"Big T said no drinking and no whoring. I'm not about to cross him."

Utah shook his head with exasperation. "That ain't what I was a'getting at, ya horse's ass. If anyone has seen a stranger come through here, it'd be one of the two or both. We'll let Whiskers go an' ask questions since people don't get their hackles up around him. Whiskers, see that bend in the lil' creek yonder? The rest of us will be there watering the horses. When you've asked around, meet us there. Don't forget to stop at that lil' store, either."

"Sure thing, Utah."

They started riding out of the trees and toward the town.

Clap was particularly fond of kicking his chair back on two legs against the wall of the stable and soaking in the sunshine while he watched the few patrons of the town going about their business. Mrs. Farrin was across the street in her flower garden, weeding and fussing over them. Presently, he was contemplating why anyone would put so much time and effort into flowers. He could understand a vegetable garden, but what good are flowers? It must be a woman thing, he thought to himself. Movement caught the corner of his eye, and he looked out towards the trail coming through the valley and into town. He was in time to see three horsemen break off towards the creek. One rider kept coming towards town. He watched as the horse plodded up the street and stopped in front of him. "Howdy. Somethin' I kin do fer ya?" The man he was addressing was about his age. His chin and cheeks were covered in a thin layer of whiskers. He had thin hair, cut short, which was a silver grey and parted naturally to the right. He was thin and short, and sitting there on his horse, it looked too big for him. It was almost comical.

Whiskers gave Clap a big, genuine, toothless smile, and his eyes sparkled with delight. "Howdy, friend! Seems like a right pleasant an' comfortable lil' town y'all got tucked away here between the hills! Funny, ya travel along a trail an' ya just don't expect to come upon some'tin so purty up ahead."

Clap immediately liked the personable little man, but his thoughts kept going back to the other three riders that disappeared down towards the creek. "Yeah, it's a purty lil' place. Not sure I would call it friendly. We don't get many strays this way. Mind me askin' what brings ya way out here? Iffn' it's none of my business, go ahead and tell me to mind my own beeswax!" He gave whiskers a wide, friendly smile back.

"Oh, well I'm glad ya asked! I'm looking fer a couple of pards of mine. They're out galavantin' the countryside somewhar' an' I thought maybe they might of come through here. Names are Riff an' Trey. Riff rides a chestnut with three white socks, and Trey's hoss is dark brown an' has a white nose and a white mane."

Clap recognized the descriptions of the horses. They were the horses Titche brought in and gave to the T Double Box ranch. He scratched his head while he gazed at Whiskers. "Can't say as I've seen two men traveling ta'gether come through here. We're pretty remote. Not a lot of travelers this a'way." Whiskers' smile faltered a little, just a little. If a body wasn't already a little suspicious of the tiny man, it would probably go unnoticed, but Clap noticed because Clap was suspicious. He glanced out where the other three riders had disappeared.

"Huh. Ain't that some'tin. I thought fer sure they came this a'way. I sure hope nuttin bad happened to 'em. They was agreeable sorts. A no-gooder could'a taken advantage of em', killed 'em, an' stole their hosses an' what lil' bit of money they carried."

"Yep, yep. Things like that always kin happen an' have. Doesn't it make ya worry, riden' around by yer lonesome like ya are?" Clap was studying the little fellow. He didn't seem like an outlaw, but he didn't seem right either.

Whiskers wetted his lips and tried another engaging smile again. "Sure, I worry! But I'm a pretty careful man an,' of course iffn' I could find my pards, there'd be three of us and I'd be a lot safer."

Clap had set a trap and he had caught a polecat. He lied about being alone. Anyone who lied about something, couldn't be trusted for anything. He remembered his promise to Titche. Those outlaws had friends. That's what he had said. Clap believed these were at least some of those friends. "Well, iffn' yer planin' on campin' outside'a town, ya should be purty safe. No reason fer outlaws ta ride this a'way. Nothin' fer 'em to steal. We ain't got a bank, hotel, or even an eatery!"

Whiskers sat his horse for a minute. He had a feeling the hostler knew more than he was saying, but he didn't dare to try to pry any harder. Maybe one of the other places would be more forthcoming. Whiskers looked dejected. His shoulders slumped, and he hung his head a little. "Thanks kindly fer yer time. I think I'll stop at the lil' store and see if they have some possibles and maybe grab a quick nip at the saloon fer I carry on lookin' fer my pards. *Nobody* has come through here recently?"

"Like I said, we almost never get strangers through." Clap touched the rim of his hat and watched Whiskers turn and ride across the road. Maybett, the store owner, had been laid up sick at the T Double Box for over two weeks. He wouldn't have a thing to tell. But Riley, at the saloon, was a different story. As soon as whiskers went inside, Clap hot-footed it through the barn and to the back of the saloon not far away. He slipped inside and told Riley what he had seen, how the little man had lied to him, and how he suspected they were some of the outlaws Titche warned him about.

Riley listened closely. He knew a little more about things than Clap did. Even though the T Double Box boys were not supposed to talk, once the liquor took hold, he heard about what happened to JW and what had happened to Titche. He knew he was on the vengeance trail. Unlike the T Double Box boys, Riley knew how to keep his mouth shut. "Thanks fer warnin' me, Clap. I don't truck with no gossip no ways. He ain't gonna get nothin' here but a shot of Devil water and the door. You better get back to the stable ore'in he might find it a bit suspicious." Clap took off like he was late for Mable's bell. Riley smiled.

It wasn't long before the little man pushed his way through the batwings like he was having a minnie-fight with them. He came to the bar and stood eyeing the bottle behind Riley, unconsciously licking his lips.

"Can I git ya some'thin'?"

He hesitated for a brief second. "Oh, no, I can't! The boss wouldn't have it."

"The boss? Is he meetin' ya here?"

Whiskers blushed. "No. I dunno why I said that."

"Iffn' yer not here fer a drink, why *are* you here?"

"I'm looking fer some pards of mine…" Whiskers went into the spiel again for the third time and for the third time, he struck out. When no information was forthcoming from the saloon either, he walked out and looked up and down the street. There was nothing else here. He would have to ride back to the boys and tell them he had struck out.

"Whadda ya mean ya struck out!" Griz looked stunned. "I never seen ya strike out ever. I cain't believe it! What's the world comin' ta? Jules, then Riff an' Trey. Now you got nothin' useful for us ta go on. An here there is someone out there preying on us!" Griz's eyes scanned the mountains. "No tellin' where, or what, the dumb son of a bitch is gonna do next. He's ghost."

Utah got up in the saddle. "Calm down, Griz."

"We don't know what he looks like, what he rides. Hell! He could be anyone, Utah. He could'a walked out on the street back there an' shook Whiskers' hand an' we'd never know it!"

Quinn had followed Utah's example and had climbed up into his own saddle. "He ain't no ghost. I'll prove it. He'll bleed jus' like anyone else when I put a bullet in his forehead."

Whiskers was already in the saddle, having just come from town with the disappointing news. Utah and Quinn turned their mounts and started walking them away. "Ya comin', Griz? Git on yer hoss already." He turned to follow the other two.

Grizzly looked at the fading backs of his pards. He shook his head and mounted up, kicking the horse into a trot with his heels to catch up. "I don't like this a'tal. I think we should turn around an' git back with Big T. Forget this feller until there's plenty more of us."

Utah looked incredulous. "First off, what d'ya think Big T will do to ya when he sees ya didn't do as ya were told? An' secondly, it's *one* man. Four of us should be able to handle *one* man easy enough! Damn, Griz, what's gotten into ya? Yer as nervous as a long-tailed cat in a room full of rockin' chairs."

They rode on, going North and leaving Fairview Valley behind, quietly soaking up the afternoon sunshine. They rode in a single file. Griz was last. He scowled as he stared at the three backs in front of him. He could feel his 'mean' starting to simmer. He didn't like this one bit. He wasn't keen on dying for anyone, even Big T. They were all quiet.

It was still early summer, and the days were long. They had ridden well into the evening hours and had long since left the lush bottomland behind. They were in a wide canyon where there was a small spring-fed pond. Since it had water and grass for their horses, it was as good a place as any to make camp and cook some bacon for dinner and maybe some beans. Utah and Whiskers talked about a whole myriad of things, while Quinn and Griz stayed quiet. Quin was always quiet, but Griz was brooding. Eventually, it was time to turn in. Tomorrow was another day.

High up the mountain was a man in the ledges. He squatted near the edge of one, elbows resting on his knees. His fingers held pine needles that he idly rolled between them, broke in half, then dropped only to pick up some more. He had been up in these ledges, exploring and getting to know the country, but also trying to see if he could see any movement down below anywhere. It was a long shot.

Now, he was studying the red dot, no bigger than the head on a sewing pin, far below. He knew it was a campfire, but who's? Was it just someone wandering through, or were the outlaws on his trail finally? How many of them would there be? He was one man alone. He had no special skills. He couldn't claim to be a sharpshooter, although given enough time to aim, he hit what he aimed at. He couldn't claim to be a quick-draw either. When the time came, he would just have to do the best he could with the hand dealt to him.

He couldn't stay up here. The higher up, the better your vantage point, but also the more exposed you are. Trees don't like to grow high up. Rocks and some brush were all this landscape offered. Tomorrow daybreak, he would come back here and see which direction whoever was down there went. Then he would head down the mountain, where there would be cover to conceal himself in. He would see if he could get on their backtrail and get a look at any prints they left behind. Maybe he could tell something from that. If not, he'd have to try to get up close and personal without them catching on.

Chapter 15: Bringing Up the Rear

Titche was on the same ledge as last night. He had a cup of coffee warming his hands. This morning, he hadn't felt a fire would be too much of a risk considering how far away the other campfire was last night and because looking up a slope hides a lot more than looking down a slope. A small boulder becomes a big blind spot when you are looking up. However, you can see just about everything all the way around it when looking down. He had never noticed or needed to know these things when he ran the horse ranch. Out here on the outlaw trail, he had learned much. He hoped he had learned enough, enough to keep him alive until it was all over.

The men below were getting on horses and heading out. He could see four. They didn't turn towards town. They headed North. In this part of the country, there was little to nothing. He couldn't see them being ranch hands. On the other hand, he knew the bunch he was after had more than four in it. He watched as they disappeared into a thick growth of trees and continued watching until, a few miles later, he was just barely able to see them moving across an open spot before disappearing again. He left the cliff and walked for quite some time before he came to a small grassy noll where Broken was grazing. He saddled up and headed out.

It was late afternoon when Titche reached the other campsite. He had left Broken well back in the trees and had crept most of the way to it. He still wasn't within sight, but he settled down on his haunches and waited. He wanted to be sure, if these were indeed the outlaws he was trailing, that they hadn't snuck back to stake out the site and try to catch him on their backtrail. It had been an hour. There had been no unusual sounds or sights to make him feel like anything was amiss. He wanted to get to the camp before it got too dark to look at the boot prints and horseshoe marks.

He walked forward cautiously, pistol pulled.

Titche walked the farthest edge of the campsite first and gradually went counter-clockwise round and round, inward toward the fire pit, studying the ground with each step. By the time he reached it, he was sure this was at least part of the bunch he was after. He recognized the big man's deep boot prints with the worn-down heel. Two sets of boot prints were lighter and newer, which also tracked. The last set was small. He remembered that print as well.

He looked out into the trees and wondered where the rest of them had got to. He didn't like it that they seemed to have split up. They could be coming down the trail any time now and he could be pinched between them like sandwich meat.

Titche went back to his horse and mounted up. "Broken, we need ta be on full alert ta'night. I don't know what these boys are up ta. I don't want ta get caught in the middle that's fer sure. They got me a'wonderin'. I've *never* seen 'em split up before. Somethin' has changed. We best figure out what." He leaned forward in his saddle and gave a slight squeeze with his thighs and Broken stepped forward through the trees.

He headed across the trail and went quite some distance before making a cold camp. It was dark under the trees, and he found a place heavy with brush. If anyone tried sneaking up in the dark, they were sure to make noise.

He was going to let those boys get a day's head start and then some. He figured to leave this new spot late tomorrow. If the other outlaws were trailing behind, they would be no more than a day behind, if he had it figured right. Which meant, if he saw no one by midday, the outlaws must have split up for some reason.

Noon came and went the next day. There was no sign of anyone. Titche and Broken started out. He was going to let the horse stretch out and cover some ground for the rest of today, but tomorrow, he would have to slow down again. He didn't want to catch up.

He was going over the lay of the land in his head. They were heading North. Paradise was Northwest of here. These outlaws always seemed to circle back around to Paradise at some point, so why would this be any different? If he rode north half the day tomorrow and broke west, he would end up on the side of a steep mountain. It would give him another vantage point. That was going to be the goal.

The next day, it was past noon and Titche was getting anxious. The tracks he was following were getting pretty fresh. Then he saw what he was looking for. On the left, through the trees, he could see the ground angling upward at a pretty steep incline. He headed up. He had to go slow. It was an exhausting and dangerous climb for Broken. He didn't want him to end up lame. Multiple times, he got off and walked beside the horse. In the end, it was worth the effort. A small brook tumbled down the hillside and off a flat rock into a thirty-foot waterfall before becoming a small pool in the meadow below. Titche could hear it, and leaving Broken to rest, followed the sound. It was very small. Six feet wide at best, and the stream was ankle deep, but the ledge was just enough of an opening to give him a vantage point.

To his surprise, the outlaws were not far below him and apparently had stopped for the night. It was a good place to stop. The stream rushed down and formed a small pool where the land flattened out. There was a small canyon meadow with plenty of grass for their horses. And with the steep cut of the mountain, it was pretty protected. Titche made sure to tuck in under the trees before any of them saw him. From there, he studied the men, their camp, and their horses, and he scrutinized the area around them before finally backing deeper into the cover of the thick trees.

He searched for any kind of ground that was even remotely level for Broken and finally found a very small area up higher, but thankfully, with the creek running through. There wouldn't be any graze, but there would be water. It would only be a hatful of grain for dinner tonight.

After he led Broken to the stream and stripped him of gear, he started to cautiously slip down the mountainside toward the outlaw camp. He arrived at it in the twilight of the evening just before the last rays of the sun were disappearing. There was precious little cover, but he had managed to get close enough to be able to hear them talking.

"Hand over the rest of those beans, Griz, ya already had yer fill of 'em."

"I'll eat as much of 'em as I wanna an' you can think about doin' some'tin about it iffn' yer feelin' brave."

A new voice piped in. "Griz, yer cantankerous and have been since we left that town behind. I don't know what's got ya so spooked."

"I told ya already. I don't like this. I feel like bait."

The new voice spoke up again. "There's four of us and one of him. As long as we stick together, ain't nothin' gonna happen ta anyone. Anyway, he might'a went ta'other way. We haven't seen a single track other than deer an' elk on this trail in miles upon miles. Maybe Big T and them have caught up with him."

Griz spoke again. "We ain't never gonna see his tracks because he's al'us behind us like a damn ole lobo wolf. I'm a'tellin' ya, we need to turn around an' go back."

The other voice spoke up again. "We ain't goin' back. We have ta meet Big T and the rest of the boys at Elk Canyon. At this rate, it's gonna take us a week ta get there as it is."

"Utah, ya sure are starting to rub me raw." Titche could hear the quiet anger in his voice. He didn't know this man but he knew he wouldn't want to push him much further if it were him.

"ya wanna go back down the trail, go back down it. It's a free damn country, Grizzly."

"I ain't goin' back down it alone! We're supposed ta stick together! Remember what happened ta Jules an' then Riff an' Trey! Big T said iffn' we had ta *piss*, someone better be holdin' yer hand."

"We ain't goin back down the goddamn trail an' that's all there is to it! There ain't a soul out here. I'm not so sure Big T was right about him not going back ta that town or maybe it was another cowpoke headed fer one of the ranches back there that found the body. Anyway, I've about had enough of yer surly whining, Grizzly!"

"Ya little cock suckin' side winder! I'll show ya what enough is!"

Then Titche heard the sound of two pistols being cocked. He wondered if they were getting ready to shoot each other. Instead, another voice spoke up.

"That's enough, both of you. One more word out of either of your pie-holes the rest of the damn night and I'll put a bullet in it."

"We all mise well tuck in fer the night. We kin figure this out in the mornin'." That was the same voice that complained about 'Griz' eating all the beans.

"Well?" Titche recognized this voice as the man who apparently pulled iron on his pards.

"Fine by me." That'd be 'Utah' thought Titche. "Whiskers, ya take the first watch. There might not be a soul around but we don't need any unexpected critters getting' the horses all lathered up. Find yer scrawny ass somewhere ta sit next to 'em an' get away from the fire light so's yer eyes can adjust." Titche pulled his colt and got ready. When 'Whiskers' responded, it would cover the sound of him cocking it.

"Sure, sure, Utah! I'd be happy ta take first shift!" Titche was already slowly circling toward the horses. They weren't far. With any luck, he could get to 'Whiskers' before his eyes could adjust to the dark. "Who ya want me ta wake up fer the next shift?"

"Yer choice. Don't matter. We all need ta take one." The horses were shifting around some, and one of them blew, but no one at the campfire noticed.

Whiskers walked out into the darkness and ran his hand along the horse's back on the end. He walked a few more feet before stopping to let his eyes adjust. He didn't want to trip. That's when he felt the cold metal barrel pressed to his temple. He went completely still. A warm body pressed up against the back of his. He felt the slice of sharp, cold metal across his neck. Then hot, wet blood slide down his chest. No sooner was his neck sliced and the same hand holding the knife pressed against his mouth to muffle his gurgling and choking. The coppery smell of his own blood on its blade filled his nose. He was being half pushed and half carried deeper into the woods. Well damn, was his last thought.

Whiskers, who was always a happy-go-lucky individual and who was never violent in his whole life, died in minutes out where there was nothing but trees and no one ever missed him.

Titche carried the lifeless body further out. He went very slowly and used a great deal of caution as to where he placed each step. He was never more grateful for adopting the habit of wearing moccasins than he was tonight. He didn't want the horses to spook from the smell of blood. He laid the body on the far side of an old log he came to.

One more down. He crept back through the darkness. His moccasins were not making any sound above a whisper. Back at the horses, he rubbed each one under their mane and behind their ears, letting them get used to him while he listened to the camp. Two of the men were already snoring. After what seemed like quite a long time, he heard a third snore join the chorus. Titche untied the bridle reins from the line rope pulled between two trees and tied off at each end. He carefully pulled the bridles off three of the four horses. The fourth horse he started to lead off. Most of the time, they will follow behind just because they have all been together for so long and were used to being together.

Titche stepped out into the open. Walking through the meadow would be the quietest way, but also the most exposed way. If he had to, he could jump on the horse he was leading and make a run for it. He was a fair hand at bareback riding. He took long, deliberate strides back toward the trail, which the camp was not too far from, listening intently to the snoring behind him for any changes. At first, he didn't think the other horses were going to come. It would figure that this was going to be the exception to the rule. But then they started to file out one by one, walking through the long grass, behind his lead.

Out on the trail, Titche walked about a mile before taking the last bridle off and giving the horse a slap on the rump. It trotted down the trail. He gave each horse, as it walked past, the same slap. Then he turned around and started back, throwing the bridles out in the woods one by one as he went. He had to get back to his own horse and be ready to ride before one of the outlaws woke up and wondered where Whiskers was.

It was hard going. The mountain was steep and unfamiliar. He didn't dare go back through the camp. More than once, he wondered if he had managed to somehow get lost, but then he heard the little stream rushing down toward the canyon and the outlaw camp. Following it, he found his way back to Broken.

They couldn't stay here. This was no place to try to fight outlaws. The terrain was too steep. He saddled up. Broken came from wild, sure-footed mountain stock. He let him pick his way back down while he walked beside the big horse. It was almost the crack of dawn when they found the trail. Titche went back down the way they had come the day before.

Daylight found them several miles back. Now that the sun was up, Titche got off the trail on the east side. The mountain on this side was not nearly as steep, and he could circle wide and high. Maybe he could see what the outlaws were up to.

Chapter 16: The Game is Afoot

Quinn was the first one up. "Wake up!" He kicked the bottom of their feet. They each sat up, rubbing their eyes and their jaws, looking around to get their bearings. "Did either of you yahoos take a turn at watch last night?" Utah and Griz both stood up, stretching and shaking their heads no, still looking around. "Well, neither did I."

Utah looked grim. "Where has Whiskers got ta then?"

"I don't know, but here's the other thing. All the horses are gone."

Griz and Utah spouted a string of cuss words that any western man would be impressed with. Outlaws don't like to walk to begin with and riding boots were not made for walking. Utah went to where the horses had been and searched the ground. It didn't take long for him to read the sign. Meanwhile, Quinn and Griz had come up and were reading it for themselves. "Looks like we drawed the short straw, boys. Whiskers is missing an' I'll be a monkey's uncle if this ain't dried blood on the grass."

Griz kneeled down and pulled a handful of it up. He sniffed it and his face scrunched up in a sour look. He threw the grass back down. "Damn sure is blood."

Utah was looking out over the meadow. "That ballsy bastard took those horses right across this meadow in plain sight an' none of the wiser. We better get after 'em. We'll be half a day trying to catch up with those four-legged flea bags."

Griz stood up. He looked dumbfounded. "Aren't we gonna go look fer Whiskers?"

Utah shook his head. "Yer momma beat ya on the head with a broom when ya was growin' up? NO, we ain't gonna go looking fer Whiskers. He's deader than one of Custard's injuns. There ain't nothin' we kin do fer him now. We need our goddamn horses. That's what we gotta find. An' I hope that yellow bellied jack rabbit is with 'em, by god, because I'm gonna string him up to one of them an' spend the next three days making him wish he hadn't been born." Utah stocked out of camp and headed for the trial. Griz and Quinn looked at each other, then followed

Out at the trail, they could see where the horses went north, but they could also see what looked like injun tracks headed south. Rattled, they milled around back and forth, trying to understand the sign they were reading.

"It tweren't a white man at'all. It was a damn red skin that took our hosses!"

Utah looked at Griz in pure exasperation. "Yer dumber than a frog stuck in a cow paddy thinkin' it was a mud hole! No damned injun took the horses an' then *walked* back. This peckerwood took the horses north an' probably turned 'em loose an' then had to walk back to his own. He's prob'ly hopin' we'll split up agin. Yer right about one thing, Griz, he is on our backtrail. I woulda jus taken the horses with me. He's got us at a disadvantage already, us bein; afoot an' all."

Quin smiled. "He's buying time."

"Buying time?"

"Yeah. We have to go get the horses and come back to look for him. That gives him time to get to a good place to fight from. He will have the advantage anyway."

Utah looked at Quinn. "Ya never say much, but when ya do? Ya talk like a scholar. Let's start hoofin' it after the damn hay makers."

Their feet were sore and their tempers were running hot. They had walked almost two miles. They could tell by the marks on the trail that the horses had slowed down to a walk at this point, so they probably weren't much further. The next spot with some good grass is probably where they would all be bunched up but how much further was that? They were already pretty damn tired.

They came alongside a big boulder. The trail wrapped around it. As they came around the other side, a hundred feet ahead of them, sat a man on a big Bay facing them in the trail. He wore a black hat low over his eyes. On his thigh was a tied-down colt. Tucked behind his gun belt was another. He had on high moccasins and the handle of a Bowie showed above each. The three men came to a dead stop and just stared like they were seeing an apparition. This was not what they had expected. Time stopped for just a minute. Then hell broke loose!

Griz spit in the dirt. "Why ya sorry excuse fer a yeller bellied coyote! I'm gonna beat ya until their ain't a damn thing recognizable about ya! Yer own ma won't know ya!"

Utah and Quinn went for their guns. So did Titche. All at once, there were deafening explosions, and bullets went whizzing through the air.

Titche was not a quick draw, but he was not slow either. The exercises he learned from China had improved his reflexes and he felt calm as he pulled both guns and fired. He saw the one on the right, called Utah, fly backwards on the trail. Landing on his back, puffs of sand flew into the air from the impact. At the same time, he felt the impact of a bullet on the left side of his chest and then searing, white hot pain stabbing through his shoulder and up behind his collarbone. Instantly, his arm went almost numb. That didn't last but for a second, and then his whole shoulder was on fire. This caused him to miss his shot at Quinn. He saw the outlaw dive off the side of the trail and out of sight. Meanwhile, Griz had shot and missed, but he was lining up for another shot. The impact from Quinn's bullet caused Titche to tighten his thighs in order not to be knocked backwards out of the saddle. That caused Broken to leap forward and run straight at the man shooting at his rider. This no doubt saved Titche's life. Quinn's shot from the woods only grazed Titche this time. Cutting a furrow across his back from shoulder to shoulder. Grizzley's second shot at him was a clean miss by a country mile. Titche shot again at Griz and saw the big man grab his thigh and fall backwards on his ass. Then Broken was jumping over Utah and racing around the boulder and down the trail. Titche clung to the horse with his one good arm.

Two miles down the trail, Titche slowed Broken to a walk and, after another mile, got off the trail. He headed for the high country. He had to see how badly he was shot and find a way to stop the bleeding. Broken climbed higher and higher through the trees. After several hours, they came to a bowl high on the mountain slope with one narrow opening through which they threaded. Titche pulled the big horse to a stop and gingerly got down. He pulled his gear off and rubbed the horse's neck and behind his ears before walking around him to see if he had gotten injured during the gun battle. There was not a scratch on him. "Good horse, Broken. You're one in a million." He patted him and then gave him a light slap on his rump. He watched as Broken walked out into the tall grass where he laid down and rolled a few times before getting up to graze.

Titche looked over the narrow opening. The right looked like the better option. He could see where the trees gave way to a smattering of boulders and rock before it dipped back down the other side of this arm of the mountain top. That would give him a clear view of the entrance and the bowl. He needed to be up there where he could see someone trying to come through. Those outlaws would be after him as soon as they could manage it. All but one, anyway. He searched around and finally found a faint, narrow trail. It was no doubt a game trail, probably made by deer. He grabbed what he needed from his gear and headed up. On his way up, he cut some chunks from some young birch trees.

When he came out at the rocky outcropping he saw from below, he became aware of two things. One good, one bad. These were big slabs of rock covered with rubble, creating multiple caves, any of which would make good shelter. The bad news was that he was not the only one who had thought that. There was bear scat around, although none of it was fresh. There were different kinds of bears up in these mountains. Some were worse than others. Titche thought of the rhyme his pa had taught him. Black, fight back. Brown, lie down. White, say goodnight. Hopefully, he would not meet up with whoever the former resident was.

Titche checked out his different options, finally settling on one that faced the bowl. If you sat outside, it had a good view of the way up to its entrance. He got a fire started and set his canteen partially in it to get the water to boil. Now he was ready to look at his wound. Quinn was a lethal gunman. He hadn't missed. He had aimed for Quinn's heart, and if it had not been for the hidden pocket sewn into his duster by the Chinese that still held the double eagles, he would not be alive. Instead, the bullet had hit and ricocheted up at a forty-five-degree angle, going into his shoulder, behind his collarbone, and coming out the back just under the top of his shoulder. Because it was a ricochet, the wound was large and ugly, with the flesh badly torn. The other problem would be trying to treat it. His resources were limited. Titche started shaving the birch chunks into fine strips and dropping them in the water until there was nothing left. He let the water boil while he cut one of his spare shirts into strips. He took the water off the fire and shoved some of the strips into it. While those were soaking, he opened the bottle of honey he had brought with him from his saddlebag. Figuring the water had cooled enough that it wouldn't burn him, he pulled out the strips, laying them carefully on the very hot stones close to the fire, except one. One strip he put over the mouth of the canteen. With his shirt and duster off and his shoulder completely exposed, he laid down on his back. He poured the liquid from the canteen into the hole in his shoulder. The pain just about made Titche drop it. He groaned, gritted his teeth, and arched his back. His head tossed from side to side, but he kept on pouring the liquid through until a little over half the water in the canteen was gone. Then he picked up the bottle of honey, pouring some of it around and then into the hole. He lay still for a few minutes. He was tired from the effort and from the blood loss. Finally, he sat up. Folding some of the strips into pads, he put them over the holes in his flesh. The rest of the strips he wound around his shoulder to hold the pads in place. He put his shirt and duster back on and banked the fire up. Lastly, he drank what was left in the canteen. It tasted strong and bitter, making his tongue numb. He grimaced but got it all down. Leaning back against the rock wall of the small cave, he was asleep in minutes.

After Titche tore out of there and down the trail like a pack of wolves had been set on him, Quinn came out of the woods. He went over to Utah, lying on his back in the trail. His sightless eyes stared up into the blue sky. His shirt was soaked in blood from the bullet that had stopped his heart. Out of everyone in the outlaw bunch, Quinn had liked Whiskers and Utah the best. Now they were both dead. He thought it might be a sign that it was time for him to move on. Griz's whining broke his train of thought.

"Jesus, Quinn! He killed Utah! An' shot me in my leg! I thought ya was handy with those colts ya wear. I ain't never seen ya miss anythin' ya shot at. Ya kin shoot the pecker off'n a black fly while it's in the air a hundert feet away! How the hell did ya miss that lobo!"

"I didn't miss."

"Then, how the hell come he ain't face down in the dirt with Utah?"

"I don't know. I can't explain it. I know I didn't miss." Quinn was looking down the trail where Titche had disappeared around the big boulder lost in thought.

Griz still sat on the ground with his hand keeping pressure on his wound, lost in thought as well.

Quinn turned and looked at Griz. "Maybe he is a ghost." Griz blanched. "We need our horses."

"Christ. I can't go hobblin' after no horses with this leg in the shape it's in, Quinn. Ya will need ta go without me an' bring me back one."

Quinn's response was to turn his back on Griz and start walking down the trail in the direction they had been originally going. The horses shouldn't be much further. But he was going to be much more cautious this time. He pulled out his Colts and reloaded them. As he walked, his head was on a swivel, watching the woods for any movement. That was how he saw the first bridle. It was caught in some bushes about ten feet from the trail. Quinn recognized it as Grizzley's. He grabbed it and kept walking. Fifty more feet, he happened to see another one on the other side. He grabbed that one too and kept walking. His thoughts were blowing around in his head like a Texas tumbleweed. He didn't miss. How could that hombre still be alive?

Then he saw the horses up ahead. They were grazing along the trail. After being left to their own devices for most of a day, they weren't real anxious to be caught. Each time Quinn would approach one, it would trot off twenty feet. He was trying not to get frustrated. They needed them. It took almost two hours before he was finally able to catch Whiskers' horse. Once he had a bridle on, he climbed up. After that, it was easy to catch another one. All he had to do was ride up to it. He caught Griz's horse next and bridled it. Then he caught his own and, getting off the one he was on, switched the bridle to his own horse before mounting that one. Leading Griz's, he rode bareback to where he had left Griz sitting in the trail.

Griz watched Quinn walk away. He checked his leg and it was bleeding pretty good. He needed to wrap something around it, but he didn't have anything. He looked all around him, then his eyes fell on Utah. He struggled up and hobbled over to the dead outlaw. He dragged him off the trail, which caused him considerable pain and made his leg bleed faster. Then he took off Utah's shirt and tore it into strips. He found a log to sit on and used the strips to bind up his leg. Now he was waiting for Quinn to get back with some horses. Everything was quiet. Griz realized he was alone. So was Quinn. There was no telling where that crazy lobo was that had tried to kill them all or what he'd do next. He pulled his Colt. Everywhere he looked, the colt pointed, until he heard horses coming down the trail from the direction Quinn took. He was relieved when he saw his pard and his horse with him. "Hey, Quinn, I'm over here."

Quinn rode over to Griz who was sitting on a log. He looked his leg up and down. "You'll probably need that log to get on. We'll have to ride bareback back to camp, where our gear is." Quinn paused. "Is that Utah's shirt?"

"I needed it more'n him. Ya got somethin' to say about it?" Griz looked as mean as he sounded.

Quinn turned his horse and headed for camp. When Griz was finally able to mount his own, he did the same.

Back at camp, they got their gear together and riffled through Utah's and Whiskers', helping themselves to anything they took a fancy to. They split the money they found evenly between them. Saddled and ready to go, they went south down the trail following the tracks of Titche's fleeing horse. They weren't hard to follow until he left the trail. That slowed the outlaws down a little. Since he was not trying to cover his tracks, most of the time they were easy enough to see.

It was getting dark. They would not be able to follow the tracks much longer, so Quinn and Griz made camp. They would catch up with this cowboy tomorrow, and he would not be long for this world after they did.

Not far away, Titche slept restlessly and groaned from the pain in his shoulder. His flesh around the shoulder wound was slowly becoming hot, and his flesh where the bullet had grazed his back was already hot. Titche woke off and on, thirstily drinking water from his spare canteen. This was why he was not awake early the next morning to see the two outlaws sneaking up on him.

Chapter 17: The Hunters and The Hunted

Quinn was awake early. He kicked Griz's feet as was his habit when he was waking up the other men in the camp. Griz came awake immediately, snarling from the pain shooting through his wounded leg. "Ya sorry bastard, wha'd ya do that fer!" His leg had started to swell during the night and felt like a blacksmith's furnace. His bandages were uncomfortably tight.

Quinn smirked. "Get up, sleeping beauty. Grab some hard tack and let's go."

They chewed on salted beef strips while they saddled and loaded their gear. The early morning sun was stretching its rays across the mountain tops like long fingers caressing the beauty below. Everything was lit up in shades of purple and dark greens on the surrounding mountains. Closer, vivid greens sparkled with dewdrops left over from the night before. The outlaws didn't notice any of it. They had killing on their mind and images of bright red blood in their thoughts.

They were still following Titche's trail, riding carefully. They rode slowly and quietly, their gazes swinging from side to side. Their nerves were stretched tight, waiting for trouble that was sure to come.

The terrain was changing. Everything was getting steeper, and there were rocky outcrops popping up all over. It was good territory for an ambush. Quinn knew that he and Griz would be sitting ducks, which made the pair even more uneasy. They tried to watch everywhere at once. Ahead was a narrow gap. Quinn stopped and analyzed the situation.

"Wha'd ya think?" Griz spoke in no more than a whisper.

"I think if it were me, I'd be in those rocks up there on the right." He dismounted and tied his horse to a bush. Griz followed his lead. "How's your leg?"

"I'll manage. Ya just find me that stinkin' skunk. I never wanted ta see a son of a bitch bleed ta death so bad in my life."

Quinn moved off to the right instead of going through the gap. It was a tough climb, and they were trying to navigate a pathway up through the rock ledges. Griz gritted his teeth against the pain. Blood was dripping down his leg, leaving droplets on the leaves and smears on the rocks as he dragged it up the ledges. When he thought he was not going to be able to keep going, he saw the outcrop of rock in front of him that they had seen below. There was a faint smell of wood smoke in the air. It helped renew his resolve.

Below and behind them, the smell of fresh blood was in the air. A big head had its nose up, sniffing. Sensitive nostrils were honing in on the smell, sending complex messages back to the brain about how fresh it was and in what direction. A thousand pounds of muscle, fur, claws, and teeth turned in the direction the smell was coming from. Within half an hour, he came to the first droplets on the leaves. It followed those droplets to the ledges where it found its first smear across a rock face. It took its time smelling the blood. Then it licked the rocks once. Its jaws chattered, and its spit foamed in the corners of its jaws. It lifted its massive head and sniffed the air again. Its lip stretched away from its impressive front fangs, moving to and fro as if it could get a taste of the blood from the breeze itself. With ease and grace that belied its massive size, it bounded up the rock ledges, occasionally stopping to smell the slight breeze coming down from above.

Quinn and Griz were closing in on Titche's camp. Quietly, they crept closer. Seeing his sleeping form in the shallow cave, Quin and Griz found a spot on each side. Titche moaned in his sleep. The outlaws glanced at each other. Quinn picked up a stone and threw it at Titche, hitting him in the thigh. "Wake up, cowboy. Time for you to meet your maker."

Titche woke up with a start and turned his head to see the two outlaws standing there with their irons already pulled.

"Come on out of there, Mister."

Quinn crawled out and stood up, weaving as he did and taking several unintentional steps forward, which caused Quinn and Griz to back up. They now stood just a few feet from the cliff's edge.

Looking at the Colts aimed at him, adrenaline started to pour into Titche's blood. This was fortunate as it was helping Titche to focus through his pain and fever.

Griz looked him up and down. "Ya don't look so cocky now, Mister high and mighty. What the hell ya got agin' us anyhow?"

Titche's voice was raspy. "Ya murdered my parents, raped an' murdered my wife, an' smothered my son in his crib. Yer lower than a snake's belly. All of ya deserve ta go ta hell an' burn in its fires fer eternity an' I planned on helpin' ya along."

Keeping his Colt leveled on Titche, Griz rubbed his jaw with his free hand, brow furrowed in thought. Then his eyes lit up. "Oh. That there purty young thing a few years back." He gave a wicked chuckle as he replayed the event in his brain. Titche felt his stomach tighten with rage. "Hey, look Quinn, ya didn't miss after all." Griz had finally noticed Titche's blood-soaked bandage wrapped around his shoulder.

"Grizzley!"

He looked at Quinn. "What? I'm right here. Ya don't need ta shout!"

Quinn's eyes were big with terror. All they had were pistols, and all those would accomplish against this monster would be to piss him off worse. It wouldn't feel like much more than a bee sting to him, protected as he was by thick fur and a thicker layer of body fat. His free hand came up to point past Griz and Titche.

Both of them turned.

There he stood in all his massive glory. His enormous paw with its three-inch claws raking the dirt. Its lip curled back, showing a fang of equal size to its claws. It made a low guttural sound and dropped its head down, flattening its ears back and pushing its shoulder blades up higher. It swiped its paw in fury, and sand and stones flew at the men standing there, trapped. Then it leaped forward, and so did Titche.

Titche knew none of them would survive this Lord upon the high peaks of this vast mountain wilderness. Griz was still looking at the bear in perverted awe and wonder when Titche charged into him, grabbing hold of his shirt front, and propelling him backward and off the thirty-foot cliff. Griz's arms cartwheeled in the air as they went over together, and his pistol went flying. They barely missed the deadly snap of jaws and a powerful swipe intended to rip flesh from bone.

As they fell, blood-curdling screams emanated from above and a commanding rage-filled roar. Then all was silent, just as they hit the ground.

Quinn was young, from a rich family, and very well educated. He was smart enough to be a lawyer, a doctor, or an engineer, should he choose. But, all Quinn wanted was speed and an adrenaline rush. His mother, back in Boston, died at 81. She lamented for him every day since the day he had left, and yet, still hoped that one day her son would walk through the door and give her a big hug and a kiss on the cheek. She never knew he had already beaten her to the great divide thirty-two years earlier, and thankfully, never knew how.

Quinn saw Titche throw himself at Griz and the two of them go over the cliff just as the bear was within mere feet of them. It hesitated for only a split second before continuing its deadly charge. Quinn knew this was the end, and it was going to be a horrific one. Screams tore uncontrollably from his lungs, and the bear seemed to scream back inches from his face. He could feel the vibrations from its roar in his core. The next thing he felt was those powerful jaws closing down on his head. Its breath smelled like fetid meat and swamp water. The last thing he heard was his skull bones crunching and breaking. Then all was dark.

Griz registered shock when he saw the bear and shock again when he felt something hit him like a train. Titche's face was inches from his when the next thing his mind registered was a kind of weightlessness as he fell through the air. All of a sudden, he was sick to his stomach and he thought he was going to vomit. But before he could, there was a sudden stop. He didn't feel pain. He didn't feel anything at all. Titche's face disappeared from above him. Instead, he was looking up at a sky so blue it looked deep. It was like you could see hundreds of miles into it. Snow white fluffy clouds glided across the deepness like sailboats. He had seen one of those once... Then it all started to dim. He struggled to hold onto it, but blackness won out.

His father was a drunk who barely remembered Griz at all and certainly didn't remember his name. Griz never knew his mother.

Titche saw the ground coming fast and then they hit. The stop was bone-jarring. He lost his grip on Griz. He flew to the left, smashing his already wounded shoulder, before flying up in the air one more time to come down on his other shoulder and roll to a stop seven feet from where Griz still lay. He stumbled to his feet and walked over to him. Foamy blood filled his mouth and spilled out of the corners. His eyes stared up at the sky. He blinked once and then the light slowly faded out of them. He was done for. Titche looked up at the cliff. There was no time to wonder what was going on. His body was sore everywhere. He was sweating bullets from a fever. His muscles ached, but he turned and ran. He ran until his lungs burned and he was falling as much as he was running. He came out in the meadow where he had left Broken. The horse was close by, somehow seeming to know something urgent was happening in the woods. He snorted and pawed the ground. His ears were pinned back. Titche threw his gear on him with a speed he couldn't have ever imagined having and climbed into the saddle. He loped Broken through the entrance, headed back the way they had come.

Up ahead, he heard a horse whinny. He speared Broken towards the sounds. They, too, were nervous, blowing and stamping. Titche yanked their bridles off from where he sat his saddle and swatted them hard, although he didn't need to. They were all too happy to flee the country. Each horse split in a different direction and ran like its tail had caught on fire.

When Broken became winded, Titche brought him down to a walk to let him catch his breath. He looked behind him but saw no pursuit from the grizzly. They kept walking. There was no trail here, and Titche let Broken pick the way. A few miles later, a small stream crossed in front of them. Broken stopped and drank thirstily. Titche was boiling hot. He slid from the saddle and drank from the stream, cheek to cheek, with Broken. When he had gotten his fill, he filled his hat repeatedly and dumped the water over his head and body. Finally, he climbed back up in the saddle, and Broken stepped across the stream and walked on.

Hours later, Titche was having difficulty staying alert and not falling from the saddle. His shoulder had started bleeding badly when he flung himself and Griz from the cliff. His canteen was empty of water, and his fever raged on. His eyes closed again, and this time he couldn't open them. He was slumped forward in the saddle, concentrating on the rhythm of the horse. Lethargy started to set in, and he could feel himself sliding off his saddle sideways. He clawed desperately for the saddle horn and was able to hold on a little longer. But, inevitably, his strength waned and he collapsed, falling from the saddle into thick soft meadow grass, although he never knew it.

Chapter 18: Salvation is a Horse and a Heroine

Broken might not be a rider, but it didn't mean he was dumb. He had spent a wary and watchful night in the bowl where his rider had left him. He had smelled danger from afar. There was nothing he could do. He would not leave his rider even though he could. Being born in the mountains, in a wild herd, it would not be the first time he had faced such a danger. However, it would be the first time he had to face it alone. But in his horse's mind, he was sure that if he put up a fight and made a racket, his rider would come and join the fight, and together they would win.

The next morning, there were more smells. Broken smelled other horses nearby. He smelled the riders he used to be with before this one came along. And, he smelled the danger. It was getting closer. He was getting nervous. He decided to go to where his rider had left his things and wait there. He stamped and pawed in his anxiety and aggravation. Then he heard the roar of the beast up above where his rider had gone the night before. Broken was torn. He wanted to run for his life. He wanted to charge in and fight for his rider. And, he wanted to stay right here where his rider could find him. His brain was trying to reconcile his feelings when his rider came crashing out of the woods, which was an instant relief for him. It was not hard for him to figure out what his rider wanted to do, and he was in complete agreement. But Broken knew shortly after lighting a shuck for safer havens that something was wrong. His rider was not guiding him at all. At the stream, Broken could smell the fever and the blood on his rider. It was not good. He knew he needed help, so he headed back to the last place where he knew there were other people.

They had made it into the valley, and Broken could smell the barn smells and other horses as well as cattle. They were not too far away now, but his rider had fallen off. He put his head down, and with his nostrils close to his rider, he smelled him. He moved his sensitive nose around his head, shoulders, and chest. His nostrils gently flaring. He lifted his head back up and shook it. His rider was in bad shape. Broken knew that he needed help. Deciding to leave his rider, he flew across the meadow and slid to a stop when he finally came into the ranch yard. He reared and kicked. Whinnying and making a racket. Someone came from the barn. Someone else came from the house, and another someone followed him. Broken calmed down and watched them intently. They were making funny noises, looking at each other, and gesturing.

A racket erupted in the yard.

Jake ran out of the barn just as Sam ran from the house. Right behind him was Tareece. They all stopped in the yard and stared at the riderless horse.

"Ain't that Titche's horse, Mr. Cully?"

Tareece looked at Sam. "That man after the outlaws that killcd JW?"

Sam looked the horse over. "Yep, it sure is. I was admiring him the last time he was here."

Jake patted Broken's neck and rubbed under his mane. "Empty saddle. Ya suppose those outlaws got him?"

"I don't think so, Jake."

"Are we goin' ta get some boys ta'gether an' go after 'em?"

"I dearly wish there was time for that. Go saddle your horse. You're coming with me. There's fresh blood smeared down the side of the saddle. I think Titche is bad hurt and fell off coming here for help. We're going to go look for him and hope we aren't too late." With that, the men walked off to the barn.

Tareece watched them go and then looked at Broken. The horse stepped closer and looked her hard in the eyes. Somehow, she just knew he was trying to tell them something important, and considering the blood on the saddle, she could only surmise that he was trying to convey urgency. She turned and ran for the house. Minutes later, she had a bag in one hand and a rifle in the other. The men were just coming out of the barn.

Sam saw her and knew instantly that she had decided to come too. "No, Tareece. There may be no saving him, and there may be outlaws following behind. You're not going."

"Yes I am, Sam." It was a statement of an undeniable fact.

"No, you're not. We don't have time to argue, and we don't have time to wait for you to catch a horse and saddle up."

Tareece swung around, grabbed Broken's reins, and stepped into the saddle before anyone could say holy cow, she's gone an' done it.

That was all Broken needed. As soon as he felt the new rider settle in the saddle, he spun on his heels and lit out back across the valley. He flew like a lightning strike. His rider was so light, he almost couldn't feel her on his back.

When Broken spun and took off, Tareece grabbed hold of the saddle horn with one hand and held tight to the rifle and sack in the other. The horse stretched out, hooves pounding the ground, which was disappearing under them in a dizzying speed. Tareece's hair streamed out behind her and she leaned low over Broken's neck. It was exhilarating, but she hoped the big horse knew what he was doing. One gopher hole at this speed would mean the end to both of them.

Sam and Jake were stunned when the horse took off like a bullet from a gun. They scrambled into their saddles and tore out after Broken and Tareece, but their horses were no match for him. They could see him far ahead and still getting farther. His trail through the high grass was not hard to follow, though, so they weren't worried about losing him. They were worried about Tareece. Should there be outlaws coming for Titche, she was alone out there. But she was better than average with a rifle. They would play hell if they braced her.

Broken slowed and Tareece was able to catch her breath. Her heart was pounding in her chest. Her eyes were scanning the waves of grass ahead. Then she saw him lying there. Broken skidded to a stop just feet from him and Tareece literally jumped from his back. Were they too late? She looked into his pale, drawn face. His duster was open and his shirt was soaked in blood. She put her hand on his forehead. He was burning up. While that was not good, it was better than him being ice cold to the touch. She laid her hand on his chest and almost couldn't feel the rise and fall of it. But it was there. Faintly.

Sam and Jake had finally reached them, but she didn't look up. "He's alive. Barely." They jumped off their horses and rushed over.

Tareece had grown up in Texas, where feuds ran long and bloody. Outlaws were common, and sometimes, they were even in-laws. Ranching accidents such as rattler bites, being thrown and stomped by a bronco, or gored by a wild bull were common occurrences. You win some and you lose most. So as luck would have it, Tareece Cully knew a lot about doctoring. And, just like she knew that when Broken stared her directly in the eyes, often the only thing that determines whether you'll win this one or lose them, was time.

"Can we get him back to the ranch, Tareece?"

"Not like this, we can't. We're going to have to do some field surgery, and even then, he will have to have the saints on his side to come through. Jake, take my rifle and watch for outlaws. We're going to be a country minute here." She was unbuttoning his shirt as fast as her fingers would go. "Sam, sit him up. I need to get this off and see what I'm dealing with." Same sat him up, and Tareece slid his shirt from his body. The wound in his shoulder was a large gaping hole surrounded by angry, red, swollen flesh. She didn't even have to look at the back of his shoulder to know it went all the way through. She could practically see through it. She gently pulled him forward anyway while Sam balanced his dead weight for her. It was the same in the back. There was another wound on his back from shoulder to shoulder as well. It, too, was hot and angry. Dried blood and fresh blood, both, caked his chest and back. Unbelievably, he was *still* losing more. "I need to sanitize this and then cauterize it. He'll be bleeding out shortly if he hasn't already. After you lose so much blood, even though you have a little left, you just can't make more quickly enough. I have seen many a hand die an agonizing death that way."

"What are you going to sanitize it with? We don't keep any whiskey at the ranch. How are you going to cauterize it? There's nothing around to make a fire with and you run the risk of starting the whole meadow on fire!"

Tareece pulled some lemons out of the sack, a canteen, a bottle of honey, sewing thread with a needle attached, some strips of cloth, and a wash cloth. "The amount of pain this is going to cause could stop his heart. It's weak already. But if we don't do it, he dies for sure." Tareece looked Sam in the eyes. He stared back. Then, grimly, he nodded his head. Tareece grabbed a Bowie from Titche's moccasin and cut the lemons in half. Then she held them one by one over the hole in his shoulder and squeezed out the juice with strong hands. Titche's eyes fluttered open, sightless, and he screamed in pain.

Tareece's eyes teared up. She knew all too well how much lemon juice hurt in a cut. This must be so much worse. Titche screamed twice before he passed out again. Tareece put her fingers against his neck. She could still feel a faint pulse. The lemon juice would kill any bacteria. Now they had to stop the bleeding. This would also kill any bacteria the lemon juice missed. "I need you to pry open a bullet."

Sam looked incredulous. "What?"

Tareece held the Bowie out to him. Pry open a bullet. Then dig in your pocket and pull out one of those matches you use to light your quirleys with." Sam did as he was asked. Tareece gently tapped some of the gunpowder into the wound. Too much would kill him, too little, and the bleeding wouldn't stop. It had to be just right… She took a close look at the little black dots in the wound that resembled pepper. That should do it nicely, she thought. She held out her hand. Same lit the match and handed it to her. She put it up to the wound. There was a loud hiss, and then the smell of burnt flesh. Titche jerked and groaned long and loud but didn't stir otherwise. She grabbed some strips and folded them quickly, pressing them to the front and back of the wound. She had Sam hold pressure on the back one for her. Several minutes passed, and she gently peeled her pad back. The bleeding had stopped. "Lay him back some, almost all the way down but not quite." Sam did. She opened the honey jar and poured some into the wound before she put the pad back on and wrapped the wound securely with the rest of the strips. "Trade places with me, Sam. I want to clean out that gouge across his shoulders." They carefully switched spots. She cut some more lemons in half and squeezed more juice into the gash. Titche shuddered and moaned but stayed unconscious. She laid out a strip of cloth and generously poured honey on it. Very gently, she laid it along the wound. She put Titche's shirt back on but not the duster. The few strips she had left, she used to bind his shirt around him. She rolled up his duster and gave it to Sam. "Lay him back down gently and put that under his head. Titche's breathing was ragged, but he was still breathing. Tareece parted Titche's lips with her finger and then gently put the canteen to his lips. Carefully, she allowed water to drip into his mouth. Reflex made him swallow. She looked at Sam. "We need the wagon. Lots of hay. He can't be jostled about."

Sam nodded. "Jake, give me the rifle. Go get the wagon. Make sure there's plenty of hay and get the bedspread off my bed. Don't dawdle either."

Jake handed him the rifle, mounted up, and was gone in a flash.

"What do you think?"

"I think he's as tough as a twenty-year-old wild Texas steer. He's fighting for it. We just need to help him." She stared down at him, pale and vulnerable, but battling to stay alive, and her heart went out to him.

Broken, seeing everything had settled down, now figured it was time to see what was going on. He plodded over and put his nose to his rider. His sensitive nostrils flared gently.

"You're worried about him." Tareece reached up and rubbed Broken's face. She sighed. "So am I."

It took Jake a long time to catch horses, hook them up, load hay, and grab a blanket, but he finally made it back. Tareece was staring off at the woods, petting Titche's horse, who was hovering over him. He jumped down, his brow creased with worry. "Well?"

Tareece put her finger gently to his neck. "His pulse has gotten stronger. But, he's not out of the woods yet."

Sam came over and handed Tareece the rifle. "Jake, you and I are going to lay the bedspread next to him. Then we are going to carefully lift him onto it. After that, you'll take one end and I'll take the other and we will load him in the wagon like it's filled with eggs instead of Titche. Got it?"

"Yes, sir, Mr. Cully.

Once Titche was loaded, it was a long, slow ride back to the ranch, and late afternoon by the time they got there. They put Titche in Sam's room and propped him up on some pillows where Tareece could nurse him day and night. Jake stood by rolling his hat in his hands.

Tareece pumped water into a basin and carried it to the bedside. She dipped towels into the ice-cold spring water and put them on Titche's forehead and chest. She looked up at the men standing in the doorway. "I know it's late, but someone needs to go find me a big, healthy calf and butcher it. The meat needs to be boiled down into a thick broth, and the liver needs to be soaked overnight in a pail of milk. I'll cook it up myself tomorrow. That'll help him make blood again. Especially the liver."

Jake crinkled up his nose.

"I'll take care of it."

"Thank you, Sam. Jake, go tend to Titche's horse. That animal has been through more than we know. He needs some spoiling, and he's earned it. He may have saved Titche's life today. After that, go get some dinner and some rest."

"Yes, mam, Ms. Cully." Jake disappeared.

Tareece moved her rocker into the bedroom next to her patient. She exchanged hot towels for cold ones about every twenty minutes and let cold water trickle into his mouth at the same time she changed out the towels. Even though he was not conscious, it was reflex to swallow. A couple of hours later, Sam brought in a large bowl filled with thick broth. Tareece added that to her twenty-minute regimen. Little bit of water, little bit of broth, change out towels… repeat… It was a long and exhausting night, but Titche was still alive, so that was saying something.

Sam was always up about 4:00 AM anyway, so he went to check on Tareece and Titche. "You look worse than the field mouse the cat caught the other day. How's he doing?"

"I am plum tired. He is holding his own. We'll probably know by the end of today, or tomorrow at the latest, if this is a lost cause."

Why don't 'cha get a few hours of sleep? I've been watching what you're doing, and I can handle that. When you wake up, the liver will be ready for you to do whatever it is you're planning on doing with it."

She stood up and looked down at her patient. Over six feet and all muscle, but he was lying there weak and vulnerable as a newborn. She pushed a piece of silky black hair off his brow and sighed before leaving the room to catch a little sleep herself.

Chapter 19: The Mystery of Miracles

It had been five days since Titche had come to the T Double Box for a second time. Tareece sat in her rocker and listened to him mumble in his sleep and ramble when he was conscious. These were short periods of time, usually when Titche had to use the chamber pot. He would stare at her with sightless eyes and talk and talk. She now knew a good deal about this man and the life he had lived before ending up on this ranch in her care.

Because his fever had finally broken the day before, last night was the first night she was able to sleep the whole night through. She woke up feeling fresh and energized. Dressed, she headed down to check on her patient.

Titche was sitting up, awake, but this time it was different. His eyes were moving around the room, flitting from one object to rest on another. When he noticed her standing in the doorway, his eyes focused on her.

She could see him taking her in; it was progress, but didn't necessarily mean he was lucid again. "Good morning, Titche. My name is Tareece Cully. You are on the T Double Box ranch." She walked to his bedside and laid her hand gently on his forehead before carefully peeling off the bandage on his shoulder to check his wound. It was nice and pink and was puckering, so it was trying to heal over. Then she sat down in the rocker next to the bed.

Titche studied her face. She was a truly beautiful woman. "Broken?" She laughed, and it sounded as musical as wind chimes.

"You and that horse! You're quite the pair, you know." He looked confused. "Broken saved your life. When you fell off from loss of blood, he hightailed it here and made quite a ruckus. That's how we knew you were in bad shape somewhere. When I got up in the saddle, he flew like a Texas tornado across the meadow right back to you."

Titche shook his head. "That damn horse. I've never seen the like of 'im. He's been a miracle worker more times than I kin count."

"Well. He sure loves you, Titche. He was getting right ornery in the barn a few days ago. Sam and Jake didn't know what his problem was. They wondered if he had gotten hydrophobia." She rolled her eyes. "I told them he probably wanted to know where you were. So, I let him out of his stall and coaxed him over to your window. He was able to put his head through. Now we let him come over to the window once a day and check. He has been a very good boy since."

Titche chuckled. "That sounds like him. He's unusual fer sure. How long have I been here?"

Sam answered from the doorway. "Five days today." He strode into the room and stopped at the window, where he leaned out and yelled to Jake. "Jake! Someone is finally awake. Bring Broken over." He turned back around and stood near the end of the bed. "That damn horse is nothing but trouble!" Sam's eyes sparkled, and there was humor in his voice. "I think he'll be happy to hear you talking. I know the rest of us sure are!" Jake and Broken stuck their heads in the window. The horse nickered. "It was too damn close, Titche. You're lucky Tareece is about as close to an actual doctor as anybody could be. She knew what to do right when she saw you. Good thing she insisted on coming along."

Tareece blushed and smiled.

"What happened out there? We been keeping our eyes open for those outlaws thinking they'd be trailing you here but we haven't seen nary a one. Have we, Jake?" Jake shook his head no from the window.

"Ya won't be seein' 'em either." Titche looked at Tareece.

Sam knew what he was thinking. "Go ahead and tell us. Tareece isn't a shrinking violet." She nodded.

Titche started then and told them how he had been getting familiar with the area and was thinking about how to get back on the outlaws' trail when they found him, sort of. They just didn't know it yet. He told the whole story all they through, including how he had ambushed the one they called Whiskers, throwing himself and the one they called Griz off the cliff, and Quinn getting torn apart by the bear. "Last thing I remember properly was Broken headed full speed outta the country!"

Everyone sat there in stunned silence. Tareece was the first one to come around. "Well, Titche. You're even luckier than I first thought!" She looked around the room. "I don't know about you men, but I am hungry and ready for breakfast! Any takers?" There was a chorus of approval from everyone. She hurried from the room to get started cooking.

A couple of weeks had gone by, and Titche was healing fast. He decided it was time to see how his shoulder would do when sitting a horse or riding. He told Sam he was going to go back down the trail and see if he could find the outlaws' horses. Owning a horse ranch, it bothered him to think of them out there with gear on and no one to take proper care of them. He said he would feel differently about it if they were born wild and didn't have gear on them. He figured to be gone one night. Sam told Tareece, who tried to talk him out of it. When she realized she couldn't, she insisted that someone go with him. It was non-negotiable. So, Titche and Pitch took to the trail together. They came back early on the third day with three out of the four horses in tow. Two of them had gear on them. Titche said he had wished they could've found all four, but he wasn't as concerned about the missing horse as he had been with these two in particular, that he had not been able to strip down before releasing them to bolt from the grizzly.

Since the horse round-up had gone well and not aggravated his shoulder too badly, Titche started getting up early every morning. He would ride out to the meadow and face the rising sun and do the moves China had taught him. It seemed like a lifetime ago. Everything did.

He thought about the past month on the T Double Box as he unconsciously went through the rhythmic moves. It was not a big ranch, but it was enough to be comfortable, and no one was stressed or overworked. He got on well with the hands who came and went as they tended to the cattle. He genuinely liked Sam and Tareece.

He had even gone to town a few times and visited with Clap, Riley, and met Maybett, the store owner. And, of course, he had to partake in some more of Miss Mable's cooking.

It was a beautiful place. Everyone seemed to get along and help each other whenever they could. He could see himself living here if circumstances were different. But it was time to get back on the trail. He had already wiped out at least half of the bunch he'd set out after, and he needed to finish it. And then there was Tareece. He felt a pull towards her, and he thought maybe she felt it as well. It wasn't proper, and Sam didn't deserve that.

Between the exercise and a few light chores he had taken on, his shoulder was doing better than expected, and there was no real reason for him to stay any longer. A month was a long time to impose on such good people. A month and a week, if you counted the time he was unconscious. He would break the news to them in the morning that he would be setting out again to finish tracking down the outlaws who killed his family.

At breakfast, Titche thanked the Cullys for all they had done for him and for their hospitality. Then he told them he would be riding out after breakfast to continue his search. Tareece was adamant that he shouldn't go yet. Sam had sat quietly while Tareece had her say in the matter.

"Sam, tell him. He shouldn't go yet. Allow your arm more time to heal."

Sam cleared his throat. "Well, Titche. We love having you. It feels like you are part of the family. It wouldn't hurt anything to give that arm more time. But. I also understand your need to finish this. I know the more time that passes, the harder those outlaws may be to find. Give us a couple of hours to get you some grub together for the ride at least. We'd be almighty proud to contribute what we can to your endeavor for JW's sake."

Titche smiled. "In that case, I'd gladly take a ration of Tareece's good cookin' with me. I'll get my things together an' check my gear over fer any bad spots. I'll give Broken a good brushin' an' check his hooves. That'll give ya some time."

Tareece got up immediately and started fussing around the kitchen as Titche stood and touched his hat brim before leaving.

An hour later, Sam found Titche in the barn getting his gear organized in his saddlebags. "You know, Titche, it's a miracle you're alive and another that you ended up back here with us. I meant what I said about you being part of the family. When this is over, if by yet another miracle you make it through, I hope you consider coming back. We'd be lucky to have you. If not right here on the ranch, then at least as a neighbor."

Titche was honored. "Yer the lucky one, Sam. This is a fine ranch, beautiful country, an' ya have a fine an' beautiful wife ta go with it. No tellin' what the future holds fer me."

Sam started laughing and shaking his head. Titche was stunned. "Tareece isn't my wife. She's my sister! Matter of fact, this is her ranch. I'm just the foreman." He laughed some more before he carried on. "I came here to help her when her husband died. It wouldn't be fitting for her to be here alone, even though she is a very capable woman. I can't believe you've been here a month and thought the whole time she was my wife!" He chuckled some more as he turned and walked back to the house.

Titche grabbed the little brush and started brushing Broken. He thought about the past month. How did he not realize it? He was contemplating the reasons why that would be when Tareece came out to the barn and stood next to him, rubbing Broken's soft fur.

"I'm going to miss you, Titche. I, well, I have become rather fond of you. I hope you don't come to any *more* harm, and I would greatly appreciate it if you would come back this way." She stopped petting Broken and looked into his eyes. "Even if it's only for a visit. It would be a relief for me, you see."

Titche looked back into hers, searching their depths and memorizing their color. "I'll certainly do my utmost best ta make it back here, Tareece."

She smiled. "I'll be right out with a sack of rations for you."

Titche saddled up and led Broken into the ranch yard where Sam and Tareece were now waiting. Sam's eyes sparkled. He was smiling as he tipped his hat. "Good luck, Titche. And good trails."

Tareece handed him the sack of vittles to put in his saddlebags. She stood on tip-toe and gave him a kiss on the cheek. "Fair weather and come back soon."

Titche took one of the Bowie knives stuck down in his moccasin and cut the strings holding two of the small black stones loose that decorated Broken's bridle. He handed one to Sam and the other to Tareece. "The black glass-like coating will come off these when you steam or boil them. Be careful and don't lose them." He mounted up and took off his hat. Without saying anything more, he put his hat back on and rode off. Sam and Tareece rolled the stones in their fingers and looked at them curiously.

Chapter 20: More Missing Men

Big T and his men made it to the Cabin in Elk Canyon with no sign of the man who was hunting them either in front or behind. Big T had checked the backtrail twice to see. He had been unusually quiet, and his men were wary of what he was thinking. Big T could be like a rabid bobcat at times.

The rest of his men were supposed to be there within a few days of their own arrival, a week at most. Big T had guessed that if the mystery man was not on their trail, then he was most definitely on the other one. He was still convinced the man had not gone back to Wells Deep, the last town they had been in. He waited restlessly for the rest of his men to arrive and wondered how much trouble they had encountered.

A week later, none of the men from the other group had shown up. The ones that were with him were getting as restless and agitated as he was already. This stalker had them spooked. He heard some of their talk when they thought he wasn't around. They thought this was a bad omen. Retribution had come in the form of a man who was a ghost that could not be found or killed. Others argued that their luck had simply turned bad and run out. Either way, they whispered about cutting out. They seemed to believe this evil was attracted to him personally, and if they faded away, it would continue to dog his steps and leave theirs alone.

Big T sat alone and considered the cards he held. His vicious outlaw bunch had gone from ten down to three, not counting himself. That was some heavy losses. Finding more men wasn't that easy.

Sure, there were plenty of shady individuals on the owl hoot trails, thieves and murderers alike, but finding men willing to follow a leader without back talk wasn't that easy. And, finding men who could get along with each other was even more difficult. That was the problem with outlaws. They had minds of their own and bad tempers to go with them. It had taken a lot of time and work to get this bunch together. He had killed more than a few in front of the other men to get his point across, and the point was that he was the alpha and tolerated no argument from anyone. It was his way or dead. He would be starting from scratch again, and it would take a very long time to get back to where he was before they started getting picked off. The other problem would be finding men who had the stomach for torture. A man can shoot or stab someone easily enough, but finding men who could stomach torturing another human was a horse of a different breed, and these were the men he preferred. These men killed without hesitation and didn't need to showboat. It wasn't about reputation; it was about blood lust. Get a group of men like this together, and they leave in their wake a legacy. That legacy could cause such fear that a man would quake at the thought of coming after them because, while most men were not afraid of death, all men were afraid of torture. That was what made the Apache so successful when other tribes were quickly being decimated. No one wanted to volunteer to go after the Apache.

But there was always one, he thought to himself, one man who felt it was his duty to dispense justice and stop the bloodshed. Somehow, he had crossed paths with such a man, and now he was like a bloodhound who would track him all the way to the ends of the wilderness, until they stood face to face and looked each other in the eye. That would make it very difficult to keep up this lifestyle, never knowing where he is or when he would step from the shadows to put things right.

He was holding a losing hand.

Big T gathered the men who were left. "It seems the other men have run into trouble either with our shadow or with *someone* somewhere and drew the short stick. Otherwise, they'd be here by now. I even gave 'em an extra week. They were good men an' reliable. We have lost an essential part of our team. I heard ya remark on bad luck has come our way an' that's probably so. Every gambler worth his salt knows when the cards have turned on him an' it's time ta cut yer losses an' leave the game. We are heading ta Paradise. We're gonna rob that bank an' go our separate ways. It'll be our last job. I know the bank well an' it will be our biggest payout yet, the crown jewel." He looked each of the remaining men in the eye. "Once we're in Paradise, you men can kick up yer heels a little in the saloons fer a few days. By then, I will have a foolproof plan. After we get the money an' split it, it's audios an' a prosperous future. Be ready ta ride in the morning." Big T stalked off. The men looked at each other over the fire. No one said anything, but everyone thought plenty.

Chapter 21: Making Plans

Big T and his riders left at the crack of dawn for Paradise. From the hideout in Elk Canyon, it was a long day's ride. They were arriving just as it was getting dark. Paradise was quite large for a wilderness town. It had three main streets littered with various businesses. Several secondary streets sprawled out from those that were primarily residential homes. On the North and West, it was bordered by rich wilderness. Trappers, gold miners, injuns, and loggers favored this area. On the East were superior valleys rich with tall grasses and small streams favored by farmers and ranchers. On the South, a chain of small towns were dispersed down various trails to more populated areas. Paradise was the hub where all of these industries met and traded goods, making it a large and rich city. People of all sorts clogged the streets from cowboys, Native Americans, outlaws, Chinese, Germans, and French immigrants to miners, businessmen, soiled doves, Paradise residents, travelers passing through, and everyone in between. The streets bustled with activity. But there was only *one* bank. The other important thing to know was that there was one sheriff and three deputies.

They pulled up a mile or so outside of town. Big T leaned on his saddle horn. "You boys got enough money to last ya a week, maybe more?"

"Why so long, Big T?"

"Jesus, Dixie, ain't we normally here at least a week?"

"Well, yeah, but I thought we'd be in and out, seeing as how it's our job together."

"No. We act like we always do when we come here. How many bank robbers do ya know that spend a week or more in town before robbing it? None. At best they're there for a day or two. When the bank gets robbed, who is the first one they suspect? The new gents in town that were hangin' around an' not doin' much then left sudden like. We're gonna go in like we always do an' go ta the same places we always go. Have a good time with the same women we always play slap an' tickle with. So, drink an' gamble an' have some fun, men, but don't go raisin' no ruckus. Ti'day is Fridee. Fridee and Saturdees there's always lots of people around. I'm gonna blend in with the crowd an' start makin' some plans. By next Tuesdee, I should have one that'll be fool proof." Big T grinned. "The businesses make their deposits on Saturdees. We don't mind iffn' all those businesses make one last deposit for us before we unload the coffers, do we?" The other three laughed. "There's a small stable on the south end of town with a corral out back, Pod's Livery. Sometimes I sell him some of my more questionable horses. He's a bit of a shady character. Tuesdee mornin', you boys be there by the corral. We'll go over the plan." Everyone nodded. "Alright, let's go." They trotted into Paradise shortly after.

Dixie, Lefty, and Sack headed for the crowded saloons.

Big T headed down a back street to a privately owned home. It was owned by a widowed woman who rented out rooms and provided meals in order to support herself and her daughter. She believed Big T to be a wealthy rancher. She had eyes for him, but he was more interested in her young, beautiful, and innocent daughter. Although he made sure not to let on. If everything went right, that would be another thing he would soon be stealing. He had imagined many times what it would be like to educate her in the ways of men and teach her obedience. He knocked lightly on the door. It wasn't long before it opened a crack. Big T smiled. "Good evening, Lauralie. I was wondering if you had a room available?"

There was instant recognition in her eyes. She blushed and unconsciously patted at her hair, neatly put up in a bun. "Mr. McKenna! So good to see you as always. Please come in. Room number three is available." She sparkled. "How long will you be staying with us this time?"

"The usual. About a week or so."

"Are you here on business, Mr. McKenna?"

"I am, Lauralie. How's Abigale?"

"Oh, she is fine. Growing like a weed."

"I'm sure. She must be sixteen by now? A young woman."

"Yes, she is, but she will be seventeen in another month."

"They're a handful at that age."

"Well, no. She is a very good girl. Respectful. But, I do see that she would like to be treated more like an adult nowadays. Are you just getting in, Mr. McKenna? Could I heat you up some supper?"

"Kind of you to offer, but I am very tired from traveling. If you don't mind, I'll head straight for my room right after I put my horse in the corral."

"Of course."

The next morning, after breakfast, Big T sat on the front porch smoking a cigarette and thinking. The only time he ever smoked was when he was deep in thought, planning a heist. The first thing he would need to do is buy a wagon and a couple of mules. He'd need a few bales of hay, a bag of corn, and an empty barrel. He would park it behind the bank. That would give him a place to hide the money.

The bank opened at 9:00 AM. William Dragos would be there at 8:00 AM. Big T took a deep drag on the cigarette and released the smoke slowly. He would have to get Dragos there earlier than that. That wouldn't be hard. He would tell the greedy weasel that he had a particularly big deposit to make and didn't want anyone to see him make it or for his clerk to raise a questioning eyebrow and blather it around town. He would say it was gold. That would make him sit up and take notice. Since William got five percent of his take, he would be more than happy to let him in the back door at 7:00 AM. Then he could give him a tap on his noggin with the butt of his Colt, load the money into the wagon, and park at the Corner Mercantile. If everything went according to plan, he would be buying goods for his trip out of town while the sheriff and his deputies were having a shootout with bank robbers.

The last part of the plan would be the hardest. He needed to find a diversion and a way to frame Dixie, Lefty, and Sack. He would have to leave it be for now. It was Saturday and almost noon. The town was at its busiest time of the week. He needed to make his purchases while everyone was too busy to notice him in particular or remember what he bought.

Finding a small wagon took some doing, but he finally found what he was looking for at the Wagon Yard and bought it. Two mules to pull it was an even harder task, but he finally ran into someone who knew someone else who had mules. Big T had to wait until Sunday, when a man called Miles would be in town for church. He apparently shopped for supplies at Ryder's, the store next to the church, after services were done. Either that or he would have to ride about thirty miles out of town to go to his ranch. It was late in the day so he decided to just wait until tomorrow.

Since the rest of the evening was his, he headed to the Play House Saloon, where he would have a few drinks and play poker for the evening. Who knows, he might even see if there was a soiled dove to his liking to spend a few recreational hours with.

Big T got back to the boarding house well past dinner. He could see the disappointment in Lauralie's eyes that he hadn't spent any time sitting with her on the porch. He didn't care. In his opinion, she was plain and should reconcile herself to the fact that no one would probably ever look at her twice, unlike her daughter.

Sunday came. After lunch, Big T headed for the supply store next to the church. When he got there, he asked to be directed to a man called Miles. He found him in the back of the store looking over some new harnesses. He explained he was looking for a pair of well-bred, sturdy mules to pull a wagon he had just purchased. Big T and Miles talked at length. Finally, they made a deal. Miles would bring two mules into town the next day or the day after that and leave them at Hachett's Livery. Big T included enough money in the deal that Miles would be able to pay the hostler to take care of the mules for him until Saturday. He told Miles he would be very busy the next few days and would be in and out of town, so it'd just be easier and one less thing for him to have to take care of. Really, he just wanted to keep as low a profile as he could manage.

Big T headed back to the boarding house, where he sat back down again on the front porch and lit another cigarette. He took a deep draw and let the smoke curl out slowly and deliberately. A few more draws, and he was focused again on devising the last part of his plan.

If he got the banker there at 7:00, the money would be loaded by 8:00... What next?

He could tell the boys to be at the Corner Mercantile by 8:00. When they see him walk in, that would be the signal for them to go to the back door of the bank, and he would let them in shortly thereafter. They would rob it and ride out of town, splitting up for good. It would take a while for anyone to realize the bank had been robbed, more time to get a posse together, and then they wouldn't know exactly what to do when the tracks broke in different directions. The boys would find that believable and a solid plan. What they wouldn't know was that he had already robbed the bank.

It was almost dinner time. Big T put his thoughts away for now and headed down the street to get some supper at one of the many restaurants. Afterwards, he was going to find a poker game to get in on and have a few drinks.

Chapter 22: Marat

It was Monday morning. Just finishing breakfast, Big T stood on the porch and admired the beautiful day. He was starting to feel the thrill he always felt before killing someone or pulling off a job. From now until well after it was done, he wouldn't be able to sit still. He decided to take a leisurely walk around town.

As he ambled down the boardwalk, smiling and touching his hat brim to those he passed, a man dressed in black and riding a big black horse with one white sock caught his eye. Big T stopped on the next porch, sat on the bench under the eaves, and watched as the man walked the big black down the center of the street slowly. He wore his hat low, keeping most of his face in a deep shadow. He had two tided down colts on each thigh with silver inlay in the walnut grips. They were something any man would admire. For a second, Big T wondered if this was their shadow. The man certainly looked like he knew his business and how to handle it efficiently. Someone came out of the door of the building and stood next to him, watching the man and the horse disappear down the street.

"Who might that be, d'ya suppose?" Big T glanced at the other man.

"I'm surprised you don't know. That there is a man named Marat Montgomery."

Big T was quiet for a minute. "I believe I've heard of him, but I ain't never seen him. He's a gunslinger of some sort, ain't he?"

"Yep. He's a lethal one fer sure. He kin pull leather quicker than a rattler can strike. If ya blink, ya missed it. Hell. If ya *don't* blink, ya still've missed it!"

Big T was more than a little worried. "Wha'd'ya suppose he's in town fer?"

"Hard ta say. He comes through onc't in a while. Two or maybe three times a year, I guess. I hear tell he's got family around about here somewhar. A brother, but no idee who'd he be or whar exactly he's at."

"Really. Never heard of no brother. Is he slick with a gun too?"

"Not that I know of. I heard once he was a cowboy on some small ranch. Marat don't talk about 'im. It's said he don't want any of his enemies gunnin' for his little brother as pay back."

Big T was quiet again. The man went back into the building. Was this a coincidence? Or was this his shadow? If it was, he was in big trouble. Montgomery was no one to mess with. He had a cold, sick feeling in his stomach. He sat there for a few hours watching the street, but there was no further sign of Marat anywhere. He ran through all of the hapless victims he had killed over the last couple of years. He couldn't picture any of them being this man's brother. It was time for lunch. He would get something to eat and then go see if Miles had brought the mules in today. But, after that, it would be wise for him to lay low.

It had been a long ride. Marat and Midnight were both drained, but they were finally here in Paradise.

Marat was supposed to meet his brother in Wells Deep. JW worked on a ranch a few days' ride from there and was sweet on a little waitress who worked in the only restaurant the town had to offer. When he didn't show up, Marat went looking for him. JW *never* 'didn't show'. When he got to Fairview Valley, some of the boys from the T Double Box were at the No Name Saloon. One of them he had met before with JW. A young man named Jake. They both had the same first name, were almost the same age, and were definitely best friends. Marat had walked up to him at the bar intending to ask where his brother was. The minute Jake saw him, he pulled him out of the saloon and walked with him to a small corral. There, in private, Jake told him what he knew, which wasn't a lot, but it was enough. His brother had been murdered by outlaws. A man riding a big Bay and wearing moccasins named Titche had buried him in a small clearing along the trail and was on the outlaw's trail. One outlaw had a big Paint with an X branded on his hindquarters, and they seemed to come and go from Paradise. Marat had left immediately, and he and Midnight had not stopped much since.

He had gone back to Wells Deep and talked to the men in the saloon. They had remembered a bunch coming through who had spent a couple of nights drinking and gambling before leaving again, and they remembered the Paint in particular because it was a truly beautiful horse. They had given him a handful of names to go on. Riff, Dixie, Utah, Griz, Lefty, and Trey, but there were more.

He retraced his way back up the trail, going very slowly until he finally found the little clearing Jake had mentioned. His brother's grave was there, alright, undisturbed. A cut rope still hung from a hardwood tree. There was a little campfire ring with the coals in it long since gone cold. Marat spent the night there and most of the next day, mourning the loss of his little brother, who was so young and such a happy-go-lucky sort.

They had grown up poor, and when their parents died of pneumonia just months apart, poor didn't seem so bad. Homeless and starving, Marat knew he needed to do something so they could eat. Cuddled together on a boardwalk, shivering, Marat noticed a big man coming out of the saloon across the street. He had seen him on a wanted poster pinned to the side of the very building they huddled against. "Big John Hicks, Dead or Alive," the poster had said, with a reward of $200.00 on the bottom. Marat whispered to his little brother. "Stay here, Jake Wyatt. I'll be right back." He left the shivering, rag-covered bones of his brother and slipped into the alley where whiskey bottles littered the ground. Marat picked one up by the neck that was broken in such a way that half it's diameter was missing along with the bottom.

He caught up with the man who was staggering his way to the next saloon and tugged on the back of his jacket. "Big John?" He could still remember the sour smell of the man's breath and the dour look on his face as he asked, "What do ya want, kid?" Marat drove the broken glass into the man's windpipe and backed away. The man was shocked. He took a few lurching steps towards him and then collapsed. He was the first man Marat ever killed. He was fourteen at the time. Marat yelled across the street to his little brother and told him to go find the sheriff quick. Later that night, they each ate a big meal and slept in a warm bed. The next day, Marat bought his first pistol and plenty of bullets to go with it. He walked away outside of town every day and practiced drawing and firing until his hand hurt, then he would switch and do the same with the other.

Marat took care of himself and his brother by killing for money until his brother was old enough to get work and support himself. But, he tried to keep Jake Wyatt away from the life. He had succeeded, too. Jake was nothing like him. He was very proud of that fact and of his little brother. There was nothing wrong with being a cowboy working on a ranch. Nothing wrong with it at all, and he didn't particularly like the men who downplayed it.

His brother was too young and too innocent to die. He hadn't even had a chance to become someone yet, but Marat knew that when he did, JW was going to be one of the good guys. He was honest, a hard worker, and would help anyone happily and freely. Marat was going to make sure someone paid for killing him.

He stabled his horse and rented a room at a Hargett's Hotel, which was close by. He would catch a nap and then visit the saloons to see if he could find any information out about the men he was looking for.

Marat woke up a few hours later and felt well-rested. It was time to get some dinner. He could grab some stew down the street at the Wishing Well saloon. He had eaten there before and their food wasn't bad. He strolled down the boardwalk, taking everything in with his eyes. He entered the saloon and walked to the far edge of the bar where he could watch the door and the room in general. There were a handful of cowboys around, sipping their drinks and talking about cattle. Three of them were playing cards.

The bartender, Davey, wiped the bar down with a damp towel and placed a large bowl of stew in front of him with a half dozen fresh hot biscuits. "How are ya, Marat?"

"Howdy, Davey. Been better." He had a couple of spoonfuls of the stew. "Compliments to the cook." Davey smiled. Marat knew he was the cook. "Anything going on in town?"

"Nothin' since the last time you were here. Sanders got snakebit. Big mean mountain diamond back. Guess it was the size of a man's arm an' seven feet long. Doc Ferman amputated his leg but I hear he's still losing ground. Ferman was in here last night. He said, a big rattler like that, there's a lot of pizen an' it probably got past the tourniquet. So, they figure to lose him from it." Marat washed down the last of his stew with a shot of whiskey Davey had set down in front of him. "My Gawd but you et fast!"

135

"They need leeches. Feed him calf liver one day, leeches the next, repeat for a week. Calf liver will help him make new blood. The leeches will take blood out. Just don't take more out than he can make."

"Huh. I'll tell Ferman when he comes in tonight."

Marat went to the Play House Saloon next. He had another shot of whiskey. When he asked the bartender if anyone new had been in, he said no. He said everyone there was regulars and local. Marat left.

The next saloon was the Bad Dog. When Marat went inside, there was a fair-sized crowd. The bartender seemed less than affable, so Marat only ordered a whisky. He stood at the end of the bar watching the other men in the room talk, laugh, and play cards. A man at one of the tables called. He threw down his cards face up with a loud whoop and raked the winnings toward him.

"Damn, Dixie! This's supposed ta be a friendly game! I am finding ya ta be downright *unfriendly* this evenin'!"

"Hell, Sack! What's a coupla' dollars between pards." He roared with laughter. Sack looked dubious.

Marat's full attention was now focused on the table. Titche had been right. The outlaws had shown back up here. He thought to himself, they'd better enjoy Paradise while they can, because they will be going straight to hell from here. Marat sipped a few shots of whiskey, pacing himself. He wanted to know who else was in the bunch and where they were.

After a long evening of gambling, the table cleared out. The one called 'Dixie' had done well. His partner, not so much. The other two had lost heavily. Marat went outside and leaned against the wall, lighting a cigarette. Shortly, Sack and Dixie came out and walked along the street bickering spiritedly before disappearing into the Roquette, a large hotel.

Marat knew where to find two of them. He'd be up early to see if he could find the rest.

Chapter 23: Titche

Marat was up early and was leaning against the wall of a blacksmith's barn. Hopefully, anyone who noticed him would believe he was waiting for some new horseshoes. He idly watched the people and the street from under his hat brim pulled low over his eyes. It was as much to hide what he was looking at as it was to block the glare of the early morning sun. As he watched, he saw the two cowboys from the night before come out of the hotel and walk toward him, but on the other side of the street. As he watched them slowly making their way, out of the corner of his eye, a big horse came into view from the other direction. Within a few steps, it and his rider were in full view. Marat stood up straighter. It was a big Bay, and riding him was a cowboy wearing high moccasins. Jake had said he would know Titche if he saw him, and he was right. There was no mistaking the horse and the man. Cowboys didn't typically wear moccasins. Titche pulled up to a hitching rail not far from Marat on his right, but the two outlaws were across the street and walking in the opposite direction. Marat had to make a decision.

Titche got down from Broken and rubbed his neck, face, and behind his ears. It had been a tough ride. His shoulder ached from the gunshot wound. He may have thought it was healed up all the way, but it was letting him know it wasn't quite done yet. Titche was at the Paradise Hotel. He was going to get a room and then go see Wan.

Then he felt the barrel of a pistol poke into his back.

"Keep your hands steady, friend, and hear what I've got to say."

"Ya have my undivided attention, *friend*." Titche kept rubbing Broken.

"I appreciate you burying my brother, JW, back on the trail. I went to see him and paid my respects. You and I are on the same side here. Comprende, amigo?"

Titche nodded and felt the pressure from the colt in is back disappear. He turned around slowly. Marat was now leaning on his forearms on the hitch rail. Titche stared into light grey eyes of granite. "I guess ya know who I am, although I don't know how that'd be. But, I surely do not know *you*."

Marat looked down the street the way Titche had come. The two cowboys had disappeared. He looked back at Titche. "How about some breakfast and we'll get to know each other." He didn't wait for an answer. Instead, he stood up and started across the street to Olsen's Kitchen, which was open for business on the other side.

Titche gave Broken one last pat on the forehead and ground-tied him before following.

Sitting down inside, next to a window, they ordered. Between the two of them, they got a dozen scrambled eggs, a side of bacon, and a dozen biscuits. The restaurant was small. There were only two other people, who looked like a married couple, deep in conversation.

"My name is Marat. JW was supposed to meet me in Wells Deep. When he didn't, I went to Fair View, where I ran into Jake. Jake told me about the day a man riding a big Bay and wearing moccasins came to the ranch with news of outlaws and burying a cowboy. And that cowboy was JW. He said I would know you if I saw you. He was right about that. He also told me you thought the outlaws had ties here in Paradise and that one of them rode a Paint branded with an X. I went back to Wells Deep and asked some questions in the saloon. They confirmed there had been a bunch in and that one of them rode a Paint, and they were able to give me a few names." Marat paused for a minute as he looked out the window at the street. He was getting his emotions hobbled before he went on. "I followed the trail out and found the clearing. I saw a piece of rope hanging from a tree and his grave. I appreciate what you did for him and I will owe you mightily for it. My little brother was all I had in this world." He gulped some hot coffee to get rid of the frog in his throat. "They seemed to be headed in this direction, so I took a chance that you had it square and I came on to Paradise. Last night I found two of the outlaws, but I don't know where the rest are. I was hoping you would show up so we could compare notes, and because I want to know what happened to my brother."

"Marat. Marat Montgomery?" Marat nodded but kept eating his breakfast. Titche's eyebrows raised. "I figure there's four left. The leader with the Paint and three others. I don't know who any of 'em are. So, ya know more'n I do. As fer yer brother. I'm truly sorry. They did the same to me. They wiped out my family. Murdered my parents. Raped and murdered my wife. An' smothered my son in his crib."

Marat stopped eating and stared for a minute before a genuinely evil look came into his eyes. His voice was as cold and hard. "Diablo. I must know, Titche. I must know what JW endured. Please?"

Titche's voice was soft with compassion. "Marat, be careful what ya ask fer. Once ya hear it, ya won't be able ta *unhear* it." Seeing no change in the other man's resolve, Titche told him how he found his brother and what he surmised had happened in detail. He went on to say that, while trailing this bunch, he had seen others who had suffered the same torture, including his mother and wife.

Marat wiped his mouth and swallowed the last of his coffee. He looked out the window again for several minutes, then back at Titche. "Thank you. I know it was as hard for you to tell as it was for me to hear, but I had to know. I need some time alone. I will meet you here at 5:00 for dinner. Then we can head over to the Bad Dog Saloon. That was where two of them were last night. Fellas by the name of Sack and Dixie. The other names I was given in Wells Deep were Riff, Utah, Griz, Lefty, and Trey. Any of those mean anything to you?"

"All of 'em except Lefty." Titche went on to tell him what had happened to each of the other outlaws. When he came to the part about the Grizzly and the fall of the cliff, Marat looked like a child being read a story from a dime novel. His eyes were wide and round, and his mouth hung open just a little.

"You have nine lives, Titche. I don't believe I have ever met someone like you. Maybe when this is done, we could ride together for a bit. I'd like to hear more."

"I haven't ever met someone like you either, Marat. If I live through this, I thought I might head back to Fair View. If yer headed the same way, I wouldn't say no to the company."

Marat smiled. "Don't forget, 5:00 here." He stood up and walked out.

Titche had gotten another cup of coffee and was watching out the window. He saw Marat on his big black horse with a white sock, trotting by, headed out of town. They were about the same age but about as different as anyone could be. Marat was a wanderer, a loner, and a killer. He, on the other hand, had owned a ranch once upon a time and was settled down with a wife and child. If you had asked him back then if he could be friends with a cold-blooded killer, he would have said certainly not, but he found himself liking Marat for whatever reason. And why not? After all, hadn't he become a cold-blooded killer himself?

Chapter 24: Tuesday

Big T was the first one to the corral Tuesday morning. Lefty was next, and finally Sack and Dixie strolled up. "Good mornin' men." Each one nodded in return. "I've got it all worked out. Fridee mornin' at 8:00 AM, I want you men to be in the Corner Mercantile closest to the bank. When you see me walk in, that's yer cue to go over to the bank and around back one at a time. I don't wanna raise any suspicions. I'm gonna tell Dragos I got a deposit to make an' show him the money in my saddlebags. He'll let me in with him. I'm gonna club him on his noggin' an' let ya in the back door. We steal the money and go out the back and down the trail. No one will know a thing until the clerk shows up at 9:00 AM. Out on the trail, we split an' go four ways. It'll take 'em time to get a posse together an' when the trail splits in four, they won't know what ta do."

Lefty, Sack, and Dixie all looked at each other. Dixie was the most vocal of the three, and he said what everyone else was thinking. "That's slick as goose shit, Big T. Why are we waiting until Fridee?"

"Because it's as busy as a free whore house on Fridees. Lots of people mean we'll be less noticeable."

Dixie nodded in agreement. "Don't we need an extra hoss for all the money?"

"Yer right that there will probably be more money than each of us kin carry. But when we split up on the trail, how'r we gonna split that pony? Since we'll be in an' out before anyone knows better, we kin ride heavy. We each find a place to hide most of it when we split.

That'a'way, iffn' a posse comes quicker then we think, whoever they decide ta foller won't be weighted down an' kin get clean away. Ya kin always go back fer it in a week or two. But that'll be yer choice ta make at the bank, how ya wanna play your cards, close to the vest or all in. Ya got from now until Fridee ta think on it."

"We'll be in the mercantile by 8:00 AM buying smokes, plugs, and some other possibles on Fridee mornin'. When we see ya walk in, we wander over behind the bank one at a time an' ya let us in. Load our horses down with as much as we kin carry and then we're gone. Got it."

Big T smiled. "See ya then, stay outta trouble." The group split up and went their separate ways.

Big T walked down the back alley to the other corral that was closest to the bank. This time, when he checked, there were two Missouri mules. He climbed through the split pole fence and walked up to one. It was well tempered, and as he stroked it, he could feel the muscles beneath its skin. He did the same with the other.

Satisfied, he headed back to the boarding house where he saddled his Paint. Taking a trail not far from the back of the corral, he decided he would spend the afternoon exploring since he didn't dare to go to the Play House to gamble and drink. He was still contemplating what it might mean that Marat Montgomery happened to be in town.

Right after breakfast with Marat, Titche had headed back down to the WW Supplies Mercantile to see Wan about a salve for his shoulder. Broken was still at the hitch rail, taking in the sights and sounds. Wan gave him a small brown bottle that had a minty smell when he opened it. He would put it on after he had cleaned up some and gotten Broken settled in a stable. He left the mercantile and visited Su-Lei. All cleaned up, he found a stable near the hotel and put Broken in it. Titche took his time brushing him down. Broken enjoyed it, and it made Titche feel more relaxed, too. It also helped work some of the stiffness and soreness out of his shoulder. Giving Broken a generous portion of grain and making sure his water and hay were fresh, Titche headed for his room. He rubbed the salve on his shoulder and within minutes felt a burning sensation, but it relieved the pain almost instantly. Titche laid on the soft bed and fell asleep.

When he woke up, it was time to meet Marat for dinner. They ate at the same little hole-in the-wall. Thick slabs of steak were put in front of them with potatoes, wild onions, and mushrooms. A fresh loaf of bread and butter came with the steaks. Large mugs of coffee were set down next to their plates. They dug in, and the food was delicious.

After dinner, they walked the street to the Bad Dog Saloon, where Marat and Titche got a table in the back corner. Nursing their whiskeys, Marat spoke a little of his parents and of his brother, JW. Titche understood the underlying sadness in Marat's voice. He seemed to need to remember some of the good times they had together, so Titche listened quietly. When he was done, Titche offered up some of his own stories about his family and his own brother, Tolly, who he had not seen in over a decade. There was a certain feeling of kindred loss between them.

Marat tapped his shot glass on the table and, with an almost imperceptible nod, had Titche look at who was coming in. Titche acted like he was interested in a nearby card game but was taking in the two men standing just inside the batwings.

The men, in good spirits, ordered their drinks and immediately joined in a game of poker. Titche and Marat watched the whole room, talking a little here and there, but mostly consumed with scrutinizing the crowd and privately pondering their own thoughts about the outlaws.

This evening, Sack and Dixie's luck had crawled under a log and died. Within a couple of hours, they had lost their money. Broke, the two headed back out the door to call it an early evening.

Marat and Titche went outside, where Marat lit a cigarette, and they watched the outlaws go to their hotel and disappear inside.

"What'd'ya think?"

Marat released the smoke in his lungs slowly. Blue-grey tendrils framed his face in the lamp light. "I think we keep our eyes on them. They'll lead us to the others eventually."

"I'm of the same mind. Since my abode is jus' about across the street an' I have a room on the front corner upstairs, I think I'll put the chair next ta' the window and enjoy the night air tonight. I'm not tired and of a mind to kick my feet up and listen ta the whippoorwills."

Marat nodded. I'll get some sleep and keep an eye on them in the morning.

Big T had come back from his ride and ate dinner at the boarding house. Young Abigale had served the dishes, which were of corn on the cob, roast beef in gravy, sweet potato, and apple pie. She was tall with soft brown eyes and long, soft brown hair to match. It was braided and hung almost to her waist. She had marble white skin with no blemishes, and a pale pink crept into her cheeks anytime one of the guests gave her a compliment.

After dinner, he headed for his room. Lauralie caught him as he started up the stairs and asked if he would like to join her on the porch. Big T gave her a charming smile but declined. In his room, he lay on the bed and thought about young Abigale. He wanted her and anything he wanted; he took. He had figured out young that sweat-soaked, back-breaking, work-filled days were not for him. There were other easier ways to make a living.

145

That's when he met the Comanche with the Paint. A fine horse like that didn't belong in the hands of a no-account savage. Him and that Comanche fought for days through cover and stealth until the Comanche finally got the upper hand. Big T was tied to a stake in the sun with a wet leather strap around his neck. As the strap dried, it shrank. But he was a scrapper and always had been. After the injun rode off, leaving him to an agonizing death, Big T had thrown himself viciously in every direction until the stake he was tied to loosened enough to pull from the ground. It was none too soon. Once he was free again, he went after that Comanche. He wanted revenge, and now, he wanted that more than the horse. The Apache had taken it for granted that the white-eye had slowly choked to death, so it was easy for Big T to get the upper hand this time around. He showed that Apache how to really kill a man good and slow. He cut the Camanche down each arm and down each leg. Then he rubbed manure into the wounds, letting them fester. He propped the Comanche's mouth open with a stick and dribbled water down his throat, keeping him alive to the bitter end. That was the first time he killed someone, and as he climbed up on that big Paint, he realized this was his reward. Since then, murder meant reward. Take what you want. Now, he wanted Abigale. But first the bank, *then* the girl. Big T fell asleep, a grin tugging at the corners of his mouth.

Chapter 25: Wednesday

Wednesday, Titche caught up with Marat at lunchtime. They went to Olsen's to eat because it was quiet. "Did ya learn anythin' new this morning?"

Marat swallowed the piece of fried ham he was chewing. "Nothing. I'm thinking it's time for some persuasion. We could take them into an alley tonight when they leave the Bad Dog and see what a colt pressed against their temple does for them."

Titche fiddled with his coffee mug. "I rather not. If they put up a fight, we'd have ta kill 'em an' then the last two would disappear an' we'd never find 'em. I can't live sober knowing they're out there breathin' the same air as me."

"We'd find them. Guaranteed. It's what I do. But, I agree that I'd just soon get his taken care of now as later. We can't be sure they haven't already split up since you have killed over half of their bunch already. Any suggestions?"

Titche chewed his food in thoughtful silence. "Let's walk around town today an' check all the stables an' corrals. If we could find that Paint with the X, we'd know they haven't split up yet. We kin compare notes at dinner an' talk it over further. I'll do this side of the street an' ya do the other."

"Good idea, Titche."

After he ate lunch, Big T took a ride over to the bank and tied up at the hitching rail. He went in. The clerk recognized him. He had been in several times before to deposit money. Big T told him he needed to speak with William. The clerk tapped on his door and disappeared into his office. Big T stared casually around the little room. It wasn't long before William Dragos followed the clerk out and motioned for him to come back to the office.

"How are you, McKenna?"

Big T frowned at him. "You mean do I have a deposit for ya."

Dragos smirked. "I am fond of our arrangement."

"I'm not so fond of it. I do dangerous work an' somehow *you* get paid fer it. Do you have anythin' to report?"

"There's nothing of note. A stagecoach, but it's not carrying enough to fill your hat."

"Well, it's a good thing I stumbled across a payday while I was out. Me an' the boys found a little gold operation. He reached into his pocket and took out a small gold nugget he had carried with him for years for good luck. It came from one of the first jobs he had done as the leader of a bunch of outlaws. It was because of that job that some had stuck with him and others had joined, eventually making him so successful. Now it was time for the little gold nugget to give him one last piece of good luck.

Dragos leaned forward on his desk to get a closer look, his eyes the size of dinner plates. He was almost drooling. Without realizing it, he reached for it.

Big T snapped his hand shut. "There's more where this came from."

Dragos came out of his trance and looked dubious. "How much more?"

"Let's just say, I had to get myself a wagon and some mules." He howled with laughter at the incredulous look on the banker's face. "You kin see it all Fridee mornin'. There'll be enough there that we will never have ta work another day of our lives." Big T was trying to see if the banker was on the hook. He hoped so. "Come here Fridee morning at 7:00 AM. I'll be at the back door. We'll carry it in an' get it sorted out before yer clerk gets here. I don't need him wondering about things he don't need to wonder about or running his mouth around town." He opened his hand again for Dragos to see the nugget. "Well, Dragos? We got ourselves a deal or am I taking the wagon to a different bank where I *don't* have ta give them 5%?"

William licked his lips. "Friday, you say? At 7:00 AM?"

"Yep. It'll give us an hour ta get it into your vault and give you time to figure out how much it is so ya kin get yer cut."

"OK. I'll be here."

"Good." Big T got up and went out the front, tipping his hat at the clerk as he left. He mounted his horse and went back to the boarding house. It would be supper time soon. When he got there, he put the horse in the corral and headed up to his room. He still had more plans he needed to make regarding what to do with pretty Abigale.

Titche walked up one street and back down another. He stopped at the corrals and walked through the stables. He saw some Paints, but none of them had an X branded on it. He hoped Marat was having better luck than he was. He hoped Marat was having better luck than he was.

Marat had struck out everywhere he went. He was leaning on the corral fence at the last stable on his side, wondering how Titche had fared, when he heard a horse whinny from behind what looked like a fairly large house. Most of the people who lived right here in town did not have horses. They walked where they needed to go or used the stagecoach for longer journeys. Since he didn't have anything better to do, he walked that way. There was a very small barn and behind it an equally small corral. In the corral were two horses. One of them was a big, beautiful Paint. It was healthy and muscular. On its hind end was an X. Marat would have loved to stay and try to see who the owner of the horse was, but he had to meet Titche for dinner. At least he would have good news.

When Marat got to the restaurant, Titche was already eating. He plonked down in the chair across from him and within seconds, the waitress handed him a mug of coffee. Marat took a sip. Titche was looking at him with questioning eyes while he was chewing. Marat pulled the mug from his mouth and set it down on the table. His slow smile turned into a big grin and his granite grey eyes sparkled. Titche started to smile as he swallowed his food. "Boy, they're right. That is probably the most beautiful Paint I have ever laid eyes on."

"So now we know where three of the coyotes are. We just need the last one in the pack."

"Yep. They've been in town a while now. I bet they'll be heading out soon. Their money must be getting low by now?" The waitress put a plate of food in front of him and he dug in with gusto.

"I would imagine so. Even if it's not, from trailin' 'em fer as long as I have, I kin tell ya they have never stayed anywhere much longer than a week."

"Let's go to the Bad Dog and have a drink. We'll make sure those two show up for their usual game of poker, and if so, I think we can both get some sleep tonight. In the morning, I'll keep an eye on the Paint, and you keep an eye on our outlaw friends. Sooner or later, one of them will lead us to the last coyote."

They finished their meals and headed down to the saloon. Sack and Dixie showed up like clockwork. Tonight, Sack was all luck.

Dixie was teasing him. The two were having a good time gambling and drinking their whiskey.

Titche and Marat left while the night was still young. They wanted to get some sleep so they could be up early in the morning to keep an eye on their prey. Titche volunteered to keep an eye on the hotel where Sack and Dixie were, since he could watch from his window. Marat said he would see if he could get into the hayloft where he saw the Pinto and try to lay eyes on who owned it. With plans made, they went their separate ways.

Chapter 26: Thursday

Titche was up early and sitting in the chair not far from his window, looking out and watching the town wake up. It was late in the morning when the two outlaws came out of the hotel and headed for one of the restaurants. Titche went down and sat on a bench in front of one of the businesses. When Sack and Dixie came out, they went to a livery and saddled their horses. At first, Titche was concerned, but when he saw them leave all their gear behind, he knew they would be back. He headed back up the street and sat where he could see if Marat came back from the boarding house.

Marat was up before dawn and crept down the street the Paint was on. There were no lights on in the house. He made his way into the little barn. The two horses he had seen in the small corral were in stalls. He walked over to the Paint and rubbed her face. She was a fine animal. He climbed the boards nailed to the wall to get up in the loft, where he found a spot he could see the Paint from and settled in. It was a couple of hours later when a man walked in. The Paint nickered a greeting.

Big T rubbed the horse's face. "I know. Yer ready ta go. Been languishing here long enough." He filled his hat with grain and let the horse eat from it. From up in the loft, Marat guessed him to be 5' 11 and now that he had his hat off, he could see he had curly black hair. He had not seen his face yet. "Well, Beauty, I hate ta be the bearer of bad news but yer gonna be stuck here jus' a lil' while longer." He snapped a lead rope to her halter and led her out to the corral. Marat got a quick look at his profile, but that was it. The horse was released, and she trotted out to the middle before lying down and rolling. Big T chuckled and then left the barn.

Marat stayed quiet in the loft until he heard the door to the boarding house close before slinking back down the wooden ladder. Somehow, the man seemed familiar to him, but he couldn't place him. He had traveled to so many places and had seen so many men in hundreds of saloons, but still, he felt like this man was familiar to him. He thought about the horse. He definitely would have remembered it if he had seen it before, so he knew he hadn't. But, western men changed horses frequently. He could have been riding something different when he had crossed paths with him. It was really bothering him that he couldn't quite place him. The door was open a crack, and before Marat pushed it open any further, he heard voices. One of them was the tone of the outlaw; the other sounded like a woman. He couldn't hear what they were saying and dared not open the door any further in case a hinge squeaked.

Big T didn't go into the house. He had sat down on the porch to smoke and think. The door opening and closing was Lauralie coming out. She sat in the other chair, beside him.

"I haven't seen much of you this trip." She was looking down at her hands folded in her lap.

"I'm afraid you won't be either. I have to leave in the mornin'. I wanted to ask you if I could leave Beauty here? Maybe Abigale could look after her? I could pay you rent for the stall and pay her for grainin' each day."

Lauralie smiled and looked Big T in the eyes. "I'm sure it won't be a problem. So, you'll be back then, soon?"

"I don't expect ta be gone too long. Are ya sure Abigale won't mind? I haven't seen her around much."

"She leaves early in the morning and helps the school teacher with the children. She loves it. She dreams of having her own family one day. So, that's why you only see her in the evenings now. When she gets back from there, she helps me cook dinner for our guests."

Big T nodded. "I'm sure she will make a fine mother. I don't believe I have ever noticed a school in all the times I've been here."

"It's a mile outside of town. It's got space for the children to play, whereas in town, they wouldn't have that."

"That makes sense." Big T stood up. "Beg yer pardon, Lauralie, but I need to stretch my legs." He trotted down the steps and, taking the back street, walked a couple of blocks to the Play House saloon. He entered through the back and eyed the men in the room before going to the bar. He was jacked up in anticipation for tomorrow morning, and he couldn't just sit on a porch and wait. He hadn't heard whether or not Montgomery had left town, so he was still going to keep a low profile. After ordering a whiskey and putting it back in one gulp, he looked over the soiled doves in the room. There was a decent-looking red-head lounging near a card table. Big T walked over and whispered in her ear. She got up and smiled at him, then took his hand and led him up the stairs. He spent the rest of the day playing slap and tickle, but Big T preferred more slap than tickle.

Marat couldn't see the porch, but he did see Big T walking down the street. His back was to him. He dearly wanted to follow the outlaw but knew the woman was still somewhere because he had not heard the house door open and shut. It was almost an hour before he finally heard the door open and shut. He gave it a little more time before he eased the barn door open enough for him to squeeze through it.

He walked down the street and wandered into a couple of saloons, but he was not able to find the man he saw in the barn. Now it was almost dinner time, and Titche would be wondering what he had found out.

Titche had gotten a sandwich for lunch and had found another spot to sit and relax while watching the hotel and the main street. He saw the outlaws when they returned. They left their horses at the stable and went into a nearby restaurant. After that, they headed to the Bad Dog. It was dinner time, so he went to meet Marat.

They both got to the restaurant about the same time and sat at their usual table next to the window.

Titche didn't have anything new to report. He was anxious to hear what Marat had to say. Marat told him he wasn't able to get a good look, but from the little he saw, he felt like this hombre was familiar to him somehow. He just couldn't put his finger on it.

Titche shook his head. "I know how frustratin' that kin be."

When they finished eating, they went to the Bad Dog Saloon. They sat, as usual, towards the back of the room, sipping whiskey and jawing about cattle and horses and places they had been. Sack and Dixie were there like usual, but tonight they were quiet. They stood at the bar talking softly between themselves. A man entered the saloon and sauntered over to the outlaws. Now all three men were engaged in conversation. Whatever the conversation was about, it was obvious that it was a private one.

Marat looked at Titche. "That must be Lefty." Titche nodded.

An hour or so later, the three left. Marat and Titche surreptitiously followed. Marat watched Sack and Dixie as they went into their hotel. Titche watched Lefty as he went into a different one.

"Well, they're up to somethin'." Titche looked at Marat.

"They sure are. We best keep our eyes open."

155

"How about we watch from my hotel? That way we kin each get a little shut eye and be ready fer whatever it is they're plannin'. If Sack and Dixie move from their hotel tonight, ya kin guarantee the others will be meeting up with 'em. I'll take the first shift."

"That sounds about right. Let's go."

They headed for Titche's hotel. He settled himself in the chair close to the window. His feet were up on the sill. Marat laid on the bed and was asleep in minutes . Deep into the night, Titche shook him gently on the shoulder, and they switched. Marat noticed Titche slept restlessly, mumbling and sometimes moaning in what sounded like despair. He liked Titche. He couldn't imagine the gut-wrenching sorrow that must torment him every day over what had happened to his family. He felt it for his brother, JW, but he guessed it was not the same as what Titche suffered. These men, who could do something like that without any kind of compunction, needed to be put down like mad dogs. He thought about his brother hanging and being used for target practice. Then he thought about Titche's wife suffering even worse humiliation and his child being smothered in his cradle. The craving to kill these men could not and would not be ignored. He would feel great satisfaction in pulling the trigger and watching the light go out of their eyes forever.

Chapter 27: The Perfect
Bank Robbery

Titche was awake not long after sunup. Marat was sitting by the window watching the street. "They never came out?"

"Not yet."

"I'll go get us some eggs and coffee from Olsen's." Titche left. Marat watched him cross the street below. Shortly after, he was on his way back balancing two plates and two mugs. When he got back in the room, Marat took one of each from him. The plates were loaded down with eggs, bacon, and a few biscuits.

They ate and sipped the coffee while they watched from the window. Shortly before 8:00 AM, They saw Lefty pass by the hotel riding a grey and leading Sack and Dixie's horses. He tied them off and went into the Corner Mercantile. Not far behind him, Sack and Dixie came out of their hotel and also went into the same building. Titche and Marat looked at each other and, as one, got up and headed for the door.

Big T was up at the crack of dawn. He went to the stable and got the mules. On lead ropes and with harnesses in hand, he led them to where the wagon was that he had bought earlier that week. He hitched them up and climbed up into the seat. Releasing the brake, Big T steered the team expertly down the street to a small store where he bought several bales of hay, a barrel, and a sack of corn.

He cut the twine on the hay and fluffed it out in the back of the wagon. Then he poured half the corn into the empty barrel. Last, he put what was left in the sack under the hay close to the back of the small wagon. He climbed back up in the driver's seat. Taking off his gun belt, he stashed the weapons under the seat and then pulled the wagon into the street. He took the back street to the back of the bank. He was pulling up just as Dragos opened the back door. He set the brake and climbed down.

Big T pulled the sack from under the hay and walked to the door. "Show me where ya want this. I got a few more sacks I need to bring in."

Dragos turned and led the way. "I unlocked the vault. We can put them in there. I already have scales set up." Then William Dragos hit the floor.

Big T had made it look like the sack was heavy until Dragos turned his back to him. Then Big T switched it to his left hand. Coming up close behind the banker while they were headed for the vault, he grabbed Dragos' pistol with lightning speed and clubbed him on the back of the head. He laughed when the banker hit the floor like a falling tree. Big T got to work fast. He carried out sacks of coins, cash, and gold out to the wagon and put them under the hay. He couldn't believe how much the bank had in its vault. He had never heard of anyone else making a haul this big unless it was the army payroll robberies. But he didn't think even those were as much money as this. And he was doing it alone. This would definitely be the first bank robbery of its kind.

He checked to make sure the banker was still out cold, and he was. He might even be dead. He had given him quite the wallop. "Dragos, ya don't know how lucky ya are. I had plans fer ya that ya really wouldn't have enjoyed much. I woulda enjoyed it though! Sometimes plans change an' ya gotta make a sacrifice. You're makin' one an' so am I." He gave him a kick in his side. Dragos moaned. Not dead yet, thought Big T, but he will be soon.

He left the gun on the clerk's desk and went out the back after making sure the front was unlocked, which it was.

He got back up on the wagon and drove it to the mercantile. Getting down, he went inside.

Titche and Marat came out of the hotel across the street and moved to a spot where there was a good vantage point. Within a minute, they saw the outlaws filter out one at a time from the mercantile, saddle up, and head down the street where they disappeared behind the bank.

"Where's the last one?"

Marat looked up and down the street. "I don't see him. I think they're going to rob the bank! He might be back there already. It'll take them a bit of time. Let's grab our horses."

Marat and Titche each took off at a run.

Big T came out of the Mercantile and walked down the street and into the bank from the front. He picked up the gun from the clerk's desk and, walking to the back door, opened it. Dixie, Sack, and Lefty came in. They saw the banker out cold on the floor.

Lefty gave a low whistle. "That worked slick as fish guts."

Big T gave them an evil smile. "Right this way, boys." He walked to the vault, and they followed. He reached in and handed each man a bag filled with cash. "Go put that on your horses, and I'll get three more sacks ready. The three outlaws turned around and headed for the back door. They didn't know Big T was right behind them. As they passed the banker, Big T whipped the gun out of his belt and shot the banker in the chest. The outlaws stopped dead in their tracks and spun around. They stared at Big T in astonishment. He dropped the Colt next to the banker's empty holster and shot out the front door like the hounds of hell were after him and yelled, "They're robbing the bank! They're robbing the bank!"

Throngs of people came out of buildings. The sheriff and two of his deputies came running out of the office and hightailed it for the bank.

"We've been double-crossed!" Lefty was the first one to run for his horse. The other two were close on his heels.

Big T joined the throng of onlookers on the boardwalk.

A cowboy gave Big T the evil eye. "How come ya didn't try ta stop 'em!" Several people heard him and turned to look their way.

"I was unarmed!" Big T feigned anger and indignation. Those who had looked noticed then that he had no gun belt. No more was said about it.

Shots were fired from behind the bank, and everyone on the street cleared out, Big T included. No one wanted to end up dead from a stray bullet. Big T ducked back into the store he had just been in before going to the bank. While everyone was focused on the chaos outside, he went around the store gathering the staples he would need for his trip.

Marat and Titche came galloping up the street.

Two horses rounded the side of the bank and were headed right for them at full speed.

Bullets whizzed past Titche's head like a swarm of angry hornets. Then one of them stung him on the top of his ear. He felt a drizzle of blood drip down, tickling the inside of it. He pulled his Colt. He heard Marat fire. Then, he was firing too.

The outlaw Marat shot at flew off the back of his horse through the air and landed with a loud thwap! Two holes darkened his shirt with draining blood from his lifeless body. His face frozen in the grim realization he would never see another day.

The outlaw Titche shot at, twisted in his saddle from a slug hitting him in the shoulder. His horse did a side step at that same moment, when the body of his pard landed on the ground not far from him. He lost his balance and fell from the saddle, but his foot got caught in the stirrup. The horse dragged him through the street, and as his body bounced and rolled beside him, it caused the already terrified mount to rear, buck, and kick. Women screamed and children wailed at the gruesome sight.

Titche raced in and grabbed the reins, winding them tightly around his saddle horn. Marat came up on the other side of the wild-eyed snorting horse, and together, they got the frightened animal to surrender. Marat dismounted and released the foot from the stirrup. Titche led the horse away from the body to the hitch rail. Getting down from his own horse, he tied off the outlaw's mount and went back to stand next to Marat. The sheriff walked up as well.

"Thanks fer jumpin' in an' dispatchin' these good fer nothin' coyotes."

Titche nodded. "Did ya git 'em all?"

"Got 'em all, thanks ta you two. Marat, I know you by reputation. I don't know you, though, mister."

"Name's Titche. Ya mind if we have a look at the other two?"

"One ya mean, unless you know something I don't? Do ya know who these fellers were?"

Marat stared down at the mangled corpse. "This one I've seen in the Bad Dog. Goes by Dixie. The other one, I believe, was a fella that they called Lefty."

"Let's see if ya Know the t'other one." Together they walked a short distance down the street and behind the bank.

Big T finished paying for his purchases and brought them out to the wagon. He loaded everything and climbed up onto the seat. He glanced at the two bodies lying in the street. There would be no one left to snitch on him. No one was left who could identify him. Everything had gone according to plan. He snapped the reins, and the mules leaned into their harnesses. The small wagon rolled down the street as people were gathering on the boardwalk, excitedly discussing the big shootout. Big T grinned.

Behind the bank, Marat looked down at the dead outlaw. "This one was pards with Dixie. The played poker a lot at the Bad Dog. I believe he referred to him as Sack." Sack was now a sack of holes. Marat saw at least four of them in his hide.

A deputy leaned against the bank. His sleeve was soaked in blood. He was applying pressure to try to stop the bleeding.

"Go see the doctor. We don't want yer arm fallin' off." Titche, Marat, and the sheriff went inside. The banker lay on the floor in a dark pool of blood. Another deputy was squatting beside him.

"William al'us got to the bank at 8:00 and opened it at 9:00. Looks like he caught them dirty crows robbin' the place an' drew. His revolver was on the floor not in his holster. It's missin' a shot. He musta got one off but one of the robbers put a nail in his coffin fer sure."

Titche and Marat glanced at each other. They had seen enough. They turned as one and left by the back door. Without saying a word to each other, they both started searching the ground for signs of what had happened. The man on the Paint was not here and had not been.

"Do you see anything, Titche?"

He looked up from his search. "Nope. I don't see any sign of a fourth horse."

"Let's go check that corral."

The two men went down the back street until they came to the boarding house. They went around the tiny barn to the back where there were still two horses in the corral. One of them was the Paint. Marat shook his head. "Am I missing something? Titche, I've walked the line. I know my fair share of outlaws and I have never seen a bunch that would do a thing if their boss weren't right there cracking the whip."

"Me neither." Both of them leaned on the top rail of the corral, bewildered. Eventually, Titche spoke again. "Let's git some lunch. Then we'll take turns stakin' out this barn. He's either here somewhere or he'll be back soon 'cause no one with the sense God gave ta a chicken would leave a horse like this behind." Marat nodded in agreement.

Chapter 28: Revelation

Two days later, Big T was pulling the wagon up in a niche between two big mountains not far from Elk Canyon. There wasn't much here, so it was always overlooked. The space was only big enough to graze one horse. On three sides, it was rocky ledges going up. A small stream toppled down one side into a bog. There were a few trees for shade. Big T never overlooked anything. When he and his bunch had stayed at the cabin, he explored the area while they drank and played cards. More than once, while he was out riding, he had thought the lazy bastards couldn't get out of their own way. While he was exploring this tiny little niche, against the rocky ledges near the bog were the remnants of a massive ancient tree. Being curious as to its size, he had gotten off his horse to take a closer look at it. He found he could just barely walk between it and the ledges. If you chose to slip between the tree and the ledges, a man would find that the bottom of the tree had a crack in it big enough to squeeze through. Inside it, there was enough room to walk upright and enough room to spread a blanket and sleep for the night. Big T had seen the massive trees further west, but this one seemed to be an anomaly, here by itself so far away from the rest. Here he was again at the massive tree. He set the brake on the wagon and started unloading the loot from the bank. Sack by sack, he took it around back and squeezed through the crack. Once it was safely hidden, Big T headed for the camp in the next canyon to finish unloading his goods.

Titche and Marat deliberated each day over the mystery man with the Paint. On the fourth day, while they ate lunch and rehashed their mystery man some more, the sheriff came into the restaurant. Looking around, he spotted Titche and Marat and walked over to their table.

Marat threw down his cloth napkin and leaned back in his chair. Usually, when a sheriff came to see him, it was to tell him his kind had overstayed his welcome. "Good evening."

"Good evening. Do you two mind if I join you?"

Titche was surprised. "Sure, take a load off." Sheriff Griffin sat down and looked from one to the other. Titche could see he had something on his mind. "Spill it, sheriff."

He sighed. "I'm lookin' fer a man. Regular cowboy. Nothin' special. A little under six feet, black hair."

Titche eyed Marat, who was looking at the sheriff with keen interest. "That's not a lot to go on."

"I know, Marat. I thought ya might know him is all."

Marat shrugged. "Why'd you thing that?"

"Well, it seems the bank was robbed an' ya knew the rest of the players."

Both Marat and Titche frowned in disbelief at the sheriff. "What'd'ya mean it was robbed? Ya said we got 'em all an' since we got 'em all, the money should'a still been in the bank."

"That's what we all thought, Titche. Apparently, it was robbed before we got in a shootin' scrap with those three galoots. Now, there *was* a bag of money on each of the horses. The thing is, there was supposed to be *a lot more* money than that in the vault. Now, a man with dark hair ran from the bank right after a shot was fired, yelling it was bein' robbed. A few bystanders described him an' said he was unarmed. No gun belt in sight. I just wanna find him and get his take on why he was in the bank before it was officially open an' what happened in there prior to him coming out."

"Sorry, sheriff. All we know about for sure is the names of the men who were killed. I overheard them talking to each other at the poker table is why I know the names."

Sheriff Griffin looked from one to the other again. "I guess that's just how the dog flopped. But, if ya remember anythin' else or see a man like that around town, let me know would ya?"

"Sure." The sheriff got up and left. Marat looked at Titche. "That dog hunts. I guess we know why our mystery man wasn't part of the shootout. He had already robbed it and left his three pards holding the bag."

Titche nodded. "What'a low-down double-crossin' skunk." He took a sip of coffee. "Boy, ya gotta hand it ta him, though. That was slicker than a fox in a hen house!"

Marat was puzzled. "How'd he do it?"

"Hard tellin', not knowin'."

Marat grinned. "We'll ask him when we see him."

Titche chuckled.

Big T was on his way back with the wagons and mules. When he got to Paradise, he would sell them and buy an extra horse. He would ride out to that school and tell Abigale something had happened to her mother and she needed to come quick. He would tell her the doc sent him. As soon as they were out of sight, he'd get her harnessed so she couldn't get away and take her to the Elk Canyon cabin. There, he would spend some time taming and training her before he decided where he wanted to live permanently. Maybe before long, he'd have a passel of boys he could raise up. He'd teach them to be real men, not like most of the men out here who didn't have any brass to them. "It won't be long now, honey." Only the mules heard him.

It had been six days since the robbery. It was Titche's morning to keep an eye on the Paint. Not far behind the house and corral were some woods, and Titche had made himself comfortable under a small hardwood. It was lunchtime, time to go meet Marat. Just as he was getting ready to stand up, a man rode into the yard. Titche lingered. He couldn't be sure from this vantage, but he thought it might be the mystery man they had been waiting for. The man went into the house. Titche stayed put. Fifteen minutes later, the man came out and led his horse to the corral, where he tied it to the rail. Disappearing into the barn, he came back out with a halter and a lead. Titche watched as he gave a low whistle, and the Paint trotted over. Putting the lead on the horse, he walked him into the barn.

Marat sat alone at the restaurant. It was Titche's morning to watch the barn, but typically, they ate lunch together and then switched. Titche wasn't here yet. He was never late. Marat jumped up from the table and quickly headed out the door. He was just in sight of the barn when he saw Titche come around the corner of it and go inside. Marat ran for the door.

Inside the barn, Big T was putting his saddle on Beauty. Movement caught his eye, and he looked up, thinking it was Lauralie. Instead, he was staring into a matching set of eyes. Both men were momentarily stunned. Big T was the first to recover. "Look what the cat dragged in. Hello, big brother."

Titche stared back at a younger version of himself. They were practically Irish twins. "Tolly?" He glanced at the Paint with the X branded on its rump.

Tolly saw him look at the horse and the brand. "Ya like that? It's the brand *you* picked out fer the 'undesirable'. Fitting, I thought." He

167

rubbed the horse. "I'm surprised you even remember me." Titche just stood there, staring. "Ya came all this way, Titche. Ain't ya got nothin' at all ta say? I'm guessing it has been you on my back trail."

That snapped Titche out of it. "What happened ta ya? What have ya become? How could ya kill ma an' pa? My wife, my son?"

"A lot happened, Titche. I grew up." He tightened the cinch. "Me an' the boys went ta the ranch lookin' fer a place ta lay low fer a bit. We had just done a stagecoach job an' got a pretty fair payday. Pa got all holier than thou an' told us ta leave. He didn't want our type on the ranch. Ma sniffed an' said she wasn't feeding no bunch of bandits." Tolly rested his elbow on his saddle. His other hand slide down close to his colt. He hooked his thumb in his gun belt. "Well Titche, when yer boss of a vicious bunch of outlaws, ya can't let someone talk ta ya like that. If I had tucked my tail, hung my head, an' limped away, I woulda lost their respect. The only way yer gonna control men like them is through fear an' respect. Since Ma an' Pa only ever cared about *you*, I wasn't even an afterthought, I said what the hell? An', I let the boys with me go ta work." He paused, reliving the day. "Then one of the boys outside came in an' informed me they had just seen some pretty thing go inta the house on t'other side of the corral. I grabbed up Ma an' went to have a look." He paused again. "Imagine my surprise. My big brother got married. Where was my invitation to the wedding, Titche?" Venom laced each word.

Titche was sickened by his brother's insolence. "We didn't know where ya went or what had happened ta ya. Ya just seemed ta disappear like smoke in a strong wind."

For some reason, this incensed Tolly. "I'm sure ya all looked so hard fer me." The sarcasm was very apparent.

He wanted to hurt Titche, deep down where it mattered. He was the one who had it all, the parent's adoration, an aptitude for business, a ranch, a beautiful wife, and a son. He wanted to torture him, watch him suffer. He had lived the charmed life Tolly had always wanted, but not anymore. His eyes narrowed as he watched his older brother closely. "She sure was beautiful, Titche. I don't rightly know who screamed louder, that baby or yer wife. They both had a set of lungs on 'em. While enjoyed listening ta yer wife scream, that baby was just a mood killer so I decided ta shut him up." Tolly was watching Titche, waiting for him to go for his gun. Titche stood still, horrified by what his brother was saying. "We all had a go at her. I was first of course. Pure sugar, that one." He licked his lips. "Griz took Ma out ta the barn. He wasn't finicky about his women. Some of the boys joined him while they were waiting fer their turn with yer wife." Titche's eyes watered and a tear slid down his cheek. Tolly enjoyed watching his misery. "By the time we had our fill, they were already playing target practice with Ma. I decided to take yer wife out there, too, an' see what she was made of. Watching her dangle from that rope, feet peddling, jiggling and twisting and turning… Well, as lovely as she was, it was enough ta make a man stand up an' take notice so we had ta have a second go around, ya understand. But, time was wasting, so we hung her back up a second time an' had some fun putting holes in her. She screamed. She screamed fer *you*, Titche. Like if she holler dyer name long enough and loud enough, ya would materialize out of thin air."

Titche's tears spilled down his face. "Ya sick bastard. I outta…" He shook with his rage.

"You outta what, Titche? Shoot me? Ya gonna shoot yer lil' brother?"

It was then that a different voice answered. "No, I'm going to, for Titche and for my little brother."

Only then did Tolly notice Marat in the doorway. His guts started to quiver. Marat was a notorious killer. Those who had seen him in action had said he had one of the fastest draws they had ever witnessed. But he wasn't no slouch either. He reached for his gun. He had only just gotten it clear when he heard the explosion from Marat's gun and felt his head snap back on his neck before flying backwards into an empty stall where he slid down the back wall into a sitting position. Blood trickled down his nose and across one cheek. In his forehead, just above the bridge of his nose, was a perfect round bullet hole.

Marat kept the gun up, pointed, as Titche slowly turned around. "Titche? Don't make me shoot you."

Titche stared at Marat for a minute before he spoke. "I did fer yer brother what ya couldn't. Ya did fer mine what I couldn't even though he deserved that an' worse. We're even, Marat."

Marat let the hammer down easy and holstered his gun. "We still riding together to Fairview Valley?"

"Not right away. I need some time ta get right, I think." Titche and Marat left the barn. They walked shoulder to shoulder, light and dark. "How about we go on a treasure hunt? Maybe we kin find that stolen money an' bring it back to the bank."

"Bring it back? Are you sure about that?"

"Hell, yes I'm sure!"

Marat laughed. "Let's go find us some stolen loot." They turned onto the next street, headed to see Sheriff Griffin. Marat stopped and looked at Titche. "But if we're going to ride together, you've got to learn to shoot better. I tend to get into some awful scrapes, and I don't want to have to worry about you getting your head blown off."

Titche stood still for a minute, a thoughtful look on his face. Then he roared with laughter.